Sisters of the Forsaken Stars

ALSO BY LINA RATHER

Sisters of the Vast Black

SISTERS OF THE
FORSAKEN STARS

LINA RATHER

A TOM DOHERTY ASSOCIATES BOOK

NEW YORK

SISTERS OF THE FORSAKEN STARS

Cover art by Emmanuel Shiu
Cover design by Christine Foltzer

Edited by Christie Yant

A Tordotcom Book
Published by Tom Doherty Associates
120 Broadway
New York, NY 10271

www.tor.com

Tor® is a registered trademark of Macmillan Publishing Group, LLC.

ISBN 978-1-250-78215-1 (ebook)
ISBN 978-1-250-78214-4 (trade paperback)

First Edition: 2022

SISTER FAUSTINA WATCHED on the screen as the orbital station grew closer. She turned off the propulsion and let the ship drift into the docking bay until the skin found the airlock, connected, and made a seal. The ship jolted, and she startled, but all was well; it was still young and had a tendency to overreact to unfamiliar stimuli. Soon it would settle into itself. She restarted the gravity, and when she felt her weight again, released the moss holding her to the seat with a stroke of her hand.

The other sisters were already in the ship's central chamber, preparing the goods they had to trade—downloads of rare serials, fresh produce from the hydroponics, assembled medical kits.

Sister Varvara was making a list of vitamin supplements they needed, but she looked up when Sister Faustina entered. "Our Lady of Seven Sorrows."

"I'm sorry?"

"For the ship. After Mary's seven sorrows."

"I'll add it to the list."

"I don't like it." This from Sister Ewostatewos, as she

counted produce and removed it from their inventory list.

"Why not?"

"It's *sorrowful.*"

There were two directions this conversation could go, one personal and one theological and neither of them good. Sister Faustina held up her hand. "Add it to the list and we will discuss them all. Where is Mother Lucia?"

Sister Ewostatewos pointed toward the chapel.

Sister Faustina hit the button that released the hatch between the rooms. The chapel was lit only by the lines of bioluminescent photopores grown in the ceilings of every part of the ship. They were low green currently—the ship needed more magnesium. Sister Faustina stepped quietly down the aisle between the pews. Every surface on a ship like this was soft; it was hard *not* to step quietly. They had chimes on all the hatches because you couldn't knock. The moss underfoot whispered as it compressed and unfurled.

Mother Lucia knelt in front of the crucifix, her hands resting on her knees, eyes closed and mouth still. They had purchased it from a little station near a dusty, superstitious moon right after they had launched their newly mature ship from the yard where it had grown. The crucifix was not exactly a work of art. Jesus's legs looked more like a single flipper, and the shaky-handed carver had given Him one larger eye and one smaller. But their original had been destroyed with their old ship, and they could not very well send word to the Church for another.

"I'm sorry to disturb you," Sister Faustina said. Her words seemed to flutter out and then vanish, the silence undisturbed.

Mother Lucia opened her eyes. "We've docked."

"Yes."

Mother Lucia stood up, cracked her knuckles, and straightened out her wimple.

"Everything is set? We've completed the ship's diagnostics?"

"Yes. The only thing we won't be able to get here is calcium supplements, but that supply won't be a problem for a couple of months."

"Good." Mother Lucia sighed and stepped out of the chapel. She did not smile. She had not smiled for quite a few months now. Sister Faustina had been trying to decide whether this was because she was still new at this and trying to fit into the seriousness of an abbess, or whether it was grief and fear. She had twice tried asking in carefully worded ways and had not received a satisfactory answer.

"Mother," Sister Varvara said, "what do you think about *Our Lady of Seven Sorrows*?"

"It's on the list," Sister Faustina cut in.

Mother Lucia took the inventory list from Sister Ewostatewos and scanned it over like it might reveal to her some new secrets of the ship's physiology. "I think it sounds a bit sad."

"That's what I said." Sister Ewostatewos finished packaging the beets and carrots for transfer to the station.

"It's on the list," Sister Faustina repeated. "Could we perhaps first focus on getting nutrient supplements into the ship so it lives long enough for us to name it?"

Anchises Station was one of the largest stations in the third system. Thirty vendors selling everything from interactive pornography to refurbished tablets to vintage audiodramas skimmed from the databanks of scrapped colony satellites. Twenty ships a day went in and out. Before they had docked, Sister Faustina had examined every ship scheduled to arrive for three days before and after them for any Earth Central Governance subcontractors or any that had journeys originating on Earth. It was entirely possible that Central Governance was not aware of their existence. They had a new ship, for one. Their rescue mission on Phoyongsa III had been far from any of the main relay networks or inhabited belts. And everyone who knew exactly what had happened down on that moon was either dead, a professed sister of the religious life, or had a good reason to keep the secret. They had not even heard from Terret in months. But Sister Faustina was still a great believer in precaution.

~

Sister Varvara had a list of foodstuffs to acquire and she planned to acquire them as efficiently as possible. She aimed to do everything as efficiently as possible. She had long thought it her greatest attribute. She would never be a great orator, or possess the godly faithfulness of a saint, but her efficiency rivaled anyone she could name. Which was probably prideful to think, but it was also true.

"You're going to need more than some beets and tetanus vaccines for all this." The vendor was a potbellied man, pale like an ice chip. Sister Varvara had known he was cheap because he lit his stall only with chemical photopores so he didn't have to pay for electricity. In the bluish light, his pale skin looked infected.

She stared him down. "Have the common exchange rates for grade A fresh produce changed since we entered this planet's orbit?"

The man shrugged. "You're asking for liveship magnesium transfusions. Ours are formulated by journeyman shipwrights aboard this very station. That sort of expertise comes at a price. And we don't see many of your kind of ship coming through. It costs me rent to keep this in stock."

"Perhaps you are unaware that religious sisters swear a vow of poverty." Again, he shrugged. "Quite frankly, these prices would be ruinous to the pope himself, and he has a Vatican's worth of Earth-mined gold." Right as she said it, she bit her tongue. Too close to the bone. Too close to sentiments she should not be expressing, not out loud.

"Garlic."

"Garlic?"

"The fresh is vastly superior to the powdered and none of the fresh has come in for four months. Do you have it?"

"I have some preserved in oil."

"What kind of oil?"

"Pure cold-pressed olive. Purchased from the groves on Taurus. I can ping one of my sisters to have it brought to you."

"That'll do."

"I expect so." She sent a message to Sister Faustina to bring over three of their jars when she got the chance. The vendor held out his pad, to log her identity and the debt. Mother Lucia paused over it, but there was nothing for it—if she refused, he would cancel the transaction and be right to do so. The tiny needle stung; when she pulled her hand back the droplet had already disappeared into the self-sterilizing gel, recording her identity and the debt. In most parts of this system, you could get away without using these and retain relative anonymity. But a station of this size had the wealth and the data infrastructure to maintain access to the six different identity databases that covered the four systems.

She imagined the data zipping from the vendor's pad into the station database, skipping the queue in the communications array, flying from relay to relay until it triggered an alarm on some Central Governance ship hovering invisible in a debris belt somewhere. She imagined their ship surrounded, her sisters plucked one by one out of the station's corridors while they were separated, each headed for a different death. Her pulse clanged inside her head and she searched the vendor's face for any hint of surprise. But the pad only chimed. She leapt to her feet; the room was suddenly too small. "We'll deliver your garlic shortly. Please have the supplements transferred to dock 6E."

Supplements acquired, vitamin D for the sisters and potassium and nitrogen for the ship. Now she would have to find someone willing to sell her three months' worth of powdered potatoes without trying to charge her the yearly income of a small asteroid mining colony. Perhaps Sister Ewostatewos could be talked into devoting a few more feet of the hydroponics to tomatoes. Hydroponic tomatoes did not have the depth of flavor of soil-grown, but Sister Varvara had a wonderful tomato-potato soup recipe that had sustained her through many a Lenten season.

She was still thinking about soup when a young woman planted herself in the middle of the corridor. She held a tablet in her hands. One of those roving video-drama sellers hawking cheaply made VR and video entertainment for serial microtransactions undoubtedly. Sister Varvara had had a similar job when she was a teenager on a station like this, though this young woman seemed older. Surely she could see that Sister Varvara was wearing a habit, and therefore an unlikely mark for episodes of *The Seventeen Loves of Serena Valdez* or *Escape from the Sentient Sea!* "Excuse me, please."

The girl did not move. "Are you one of the sisters of the *Our Lady of Impossible Constellations*?"

Sister Varvara stopped short. She could deny it. She could also just keep walking. She certainly did not have Sister Faustina's knack for careful politics or Mother Lucia's talent for gentle conversation. She looked around the corridor at the blank-faced, oblivious passersby, but she knew they would not have landed if there were any known ECG agents on board. And, as far as she was aware, there was not yet a public price on their heads. Somewhere on Old Earth an entire ministry of government officers was surely debating what to do about them.

For now, though, it seemed the risk of exposing their plan to spread deadly ringeye plague across the rebellious outer systems outweighed their desire to find the nuns who had stopped it. "Why do you ask?"

The woman worked the tablet back and forth in her hands. She wore her hair in a single braid, and had on denim coveralls rolled up to mid-forearm. Absolutely unremarkable, both of those things. She had the look of an asteroid-child, tall and thin. Sister Varvara thought she might have some Chinese in her background, but there were a dozen primarily East Asian colonies in this system, which hardly narrowed it down.

"You are, then," the young woman said. "I have a letter I've prepared." She held out the tablet. Sister Varvara did not take it. She smiled, a drooping, flailing thing, and gripped the tablet tighter. "I would like to request to become a postulant in your order."

Sister Varvara was holding a crate of beets, so she could not give that pronouncement the full physical shock it deserved. How she wished this could have happened to anyone else. A soft denial, that was what this girl needed. "Why us? This is a populous station. We can't be the first Catholic order to have passed through."

"Are you still a Catholic order?"

Sister Varvara stared at her. The young woman stared back.

"I am asking you because you were the ones on Phoy-ongsa III."

Sister Varvara sighed. "You had best come with me. You'll want to speak to the mother superior."

~

Mother Lucia—she was trying hard to think of herself that way, even inside her own head, no matter how it felt like a costume handed down from someone much larger than herself—was meeting with a programmer about up-dating the ship's communications filter. His office was in the center of the station, away from any of the porthole windows. In these old stations that had been added onto over and over again, the gravity always felt a little *off* this far in. Her feet were clumsy beneath her, her skin prick-led in the uneven weight. Or maybe it was just her. Lately, she couldn't stand not being in flight. Whenever she was off the ship, out of its comforting, steady momentum, her skin itched.

"Your ship is nine months old? Is that nine months since purchase?" The programmer was a skinny little man who for some reason wore eyeglasses. She hadn't seen eyeglasses on anyone for ten years.

"Since its hatching."

"Interesting. It's very rare that I get to work on a fresh

hatchling, you know. They're falling out of style. What's the make of its communications array?"

She handed over the papers she'd been given when they launched from the shipyard. She honestly did not know what half of it meant. She was a nun; before that she'd been a doctor, and before that she was a child on a mining colony. Never had she been an expert on ships, living or otherwise. She watched the man's face as he read.

"You have a shipwright on board?"

"No. We did, but she departed."

"Your ship?"

"The religious life, in fact. Also the ship."

"Before this ship was complete with its mechanical additions."

"Yes."

"Do you know how I could tell that?" He leaned back in his chair and peered at the ship's specs over the tops of his archaic glasses. He set down the papers and tapped the cross-section of the ship on the front page. "Somebody took you for a ride. The communications array they put in is one meant for deadships. It doesn't transmit through the flesh of liveships nearly as well, and they probably charged you about twice as much as they should have for it. And it isn't meant to stand up to the corrosive environment inside a liveship. The same, honestly, goes for your emergency transmitters and your data storage. But the communications array is the most pressing concern."

A sharp pain was building behind Mother Lucia's right eye. She thought back to the last days before they had launched the new ship and all the questions she hadn't asked. "How do I know you're not taking me for a ride right now?"

"Do you have a lot of problems with garbled transmissions? Are you having to replace parts more often than you did on your last ship?"

She chewed on the inside of her cheek.

"I could just update your filter algorithm, but I would highly recommend replacing the array and data storage with models rated for the biology of a liveship. Otherwise, you run the risk of poisoning your own ship if you don't notice the parts degrading. If you let me take the old ones for resale, I can offer you an attractive price."

"And how long will that take?"

"We have a shipyard here—I can order the new models built and installed within the week."

"I'll need to speak with the other sisters about it. We make decisions like this by consensus." Also, she would have to count the coffers. She had a feeling even his very attractive price would drain their reserves now that they were outside the support system of the Church.

"I'll write up a bid." He began typing their ship's information into whatever program he used to calculate these things. Mother Lucia shifted in her seat and wished for a window.

"May I ask you a personal question?"

"My glasses?"

"Yes. I'm sorry—I was a doctor. Please feel free to tell me I'm being intrusive."

"I'm Sikh. My parents were very religious and believed eyesight was covered under respecting the perfection of God's creation, so they didn't have mine corrected. I'm not as religious, but I like them now. I like being able to take them off at the end of the day and close off the world beyond the end of my nose."

"I see. Though—I thought it was only hair?"

"It's complicated. As I said, very religious."

She nodded. "I can understand that. Out this far people practice Catholicism in many ways that the Church on Earth would not recognize."

He nodded, and finished tapping in figures. "Actually. May I ask you something yourself?"

"Of course."

He gestured at her habit. "Why do you keep with that? Surely it's impractical in zero-g."

"Dressing this way is modest, but it does have practical considerations. It gives us a measure of protection in situations where people are hostile to strangers or suspicious of us, or where most civilians would not be allowed to go. There was a time when many in our order simply dressed in modest ordinary clothing. As far as I know, many still do on Old Earth. Technically, as we do our work 'in the world,' we are religious sisters and not nuns, and can dress how we like. Though that distinction has all but disappeared." She smiled. So strange, to talk about the rules with someone who didn't already know them. "And of course, we've made modifications. We wear suits instead of underskirts like they did in the old days, and these have stickpads at the ankles and wrists to keep it out of our way when the gravity is off."

"I feel like I've been let in on a secret."

She laughed. She had forgotten what it was like to be treated like a mystery. Back when she was in her novitiate, everything had felt impossibly strange and archaic and loaded with import. Somewhere along the way that feeling had given in to the mundane. Then the programmer dropped his cost estimate into her tablet, and the lightness disappeared. "We can't afford this."

"No engineer on your ship?"

"No." Gemma would have understood how the mechanical systems had to interface with the ship's body, even though she was a biologist and not an engineer. But Gemma was gone now, off on her women's ship some-

where beyond helping them. And the prices of the supplies alone were out of their grasp.

"Well . . ." The man spread his hands, in a gesture uni-
versal for saying *I'd like to help, but you know how the economics of these worlds work.* And Mother Lucia did. Those
economics were going to crush them.

~

Sister Ewostatewos passed the station's ring, where the
shops and freelance suppliers were, and headed back toward the rented compartments. The other sisters were
already away on their errands. She told herself no one
would notice her deviation. The farther she got from the
shops and the docks, the more she stood out. Here it was
all contracted workers off company ships. Half of them
probably came from the sort of world where the company was also the government and also the law. Most
of them wore standard-issue clothing and standard-issue
haircuts, and there was a long line at the exchange to
trade company scrip for hard currency. The exchange
rates were uniformly ruinous.

She turned down another corner and the corridor
emptied. She wanted to stop, but she would already
be remembered. If anyone asked, they would recall a
Black woman in a black habit. She was a crow in a flock

of gray starlings.

She missed crows. So many colonies had brought in starlings, either to alter the ecosystem or to deal with litter in larger stations. So few had thought to bring crows. Too troublesome.

She found the door. The encrypted message had only come this morning, after Sister Faustina transmitted their identity certificate to the station, but she was sure it was no coincidence that they'd ended up in the same corner of space after all these years. She considered leaving, again. It was a big universe. It was unlikely their paths would cross again for a long time. Then she breathed in, and there it was, the smell of chrysanthemum as familiar and as out of place here as the feeling of a hot sun on her back.

She knocked. The door to the little rented room opened.

"It took you long enough," her sister said.

Sister Ewostatewos closed the door behind herself. The room was tiny. The bed was folded up into the wall, but when Eris unfolded it, it would take up the entirety of the floor. There was nowhere to look but at her sister. Eris reached out and pinched the edge of Sister Ewostatewos's sleeve. She had cut her hair short but other than that, she was exactly the way Sister Ewostatewos saw her in her dreams or her nightmares. No tattoos, no new scars, though she had expected both.

"You really did it." Eris's hand wandered up to the veil covering Sister Ewostatewos's hair, and Sister Ewostatewos pulled back. "Don't be angry with me."

"I'm not angry with you." Barely a lie.

"Of course not. It's been too long for that, right?"

There was nowhere to sit, so Sister Ewostatewos leaned against the wall, next to Eris's neatly packed knapsack. She could imagine what was inside. Two shirts, one pair of pants, several meal replacement bars, and a datastick full of trojan programs. Eris tapped her foot and grinned. That was the thing about twins. They knew all your buttons. "Why did you call for me?"

Eris tilted her head, and that grin stretched into a Cheshire cat's, like one of those cartoons from Old Earth that got auto-uploaded onto every new deadship's media kit along with the rest of the public domain database, and which had scared them both so much as little ones. "I heard you were on the side of the angels now."

Sister Ewostatewos snorted. "You're late. I took my solemn vows three years ago."

"I was talking about Phoyongsa III," Eris said, "and the meaningful kind of angels."

"How do you know about Phoyongsa III?"

"Soon everyone will know. It's been pinging all around the darkcomms net, and it's bubbling up. Soon it will break through to the media."

They'd known it would. Everyone who had been on the planet—who had seen the blood and the quiet bodies—had sworn themselves to silence, but the story was too big. Every child born since the war had grown up hearing ringeye ghost stories—how the disease hijacked your mind, made you lash out in a frenzy at all those around you, and then bled you out, all in a package so contagious that it left whole colonies and stations full of nothing but bodies. The story of another outbreak, this one the deliberate work of Central Governance . . . that was a story too big to hide forever.

The last survivors of Phoyongsa III had scattered. Many to the still-wild fourth system, where connectivity was still low and anonymity high. She should try to get messages to them. No, that would attract too much attention. They'd known it would come out. They'd just hoped for more time.

"You have come," Eris repeated, slowly, like the last lines of a homily, "to the side of the angels."

Sister Ewostatewos was silent.

"What name did you take?"

"I'm Ewostatewos now."

"That's not one of their saints. They let you take it?"

"It's one of our mother's saints."

"You don't know that."

She tried not to flinch. A trickle of that old uncertainty flicked through her, the same she'd prayed on in the cold night before she chose the name. Their mother was a few scattered memories. Her name had been Ethiopian, and her face, but whether she had prayed in any church, she could never remember. And Eris had sharpened all her own memories into weapons.

"Did you call me here to argue about the past?" Sister Ewostatewos pressed her palms flat against the cool sheet-cellulose wall, to stop them sweating. She prayed the chill to go up her spine to her head and stay her worst impulses. "Tell me what you want, Eris."

"Hire me."

Sister Ewostatewos snorted. She held up the end of her belt with its three knots. "Three vows, and the first of them is poverty, you know. We can't afford you."

"Pro bono. Tell your abbess."

"I will not bring you on board my ship." She regretted it instantly. It cut her as much as it cut Eris. Once they had been like a binary star system, conjoined by gravity, and now she had pointed out how starkly that had changed. Eris unfolded herself from the wall. She wrenched open her pack and found a meal bar. She'd always eaten her nerves. The fact came to Sister Ewostatewos unbidden, a memory from another life. "What's happened? What are you afraid of?"

"We only have one life, Ewostatewos. Don't you want to seize it?" Eris tore into the bar with her teeth, ripping off huge chunks. Her eyes were bright.

"I believe in life everlasting." She should not have come alone.

"After what we've done? Would your God let us in?"

Sister Ewostatewos wanted to say *of course,* but her throat seized up on her. Eris took her hands and twined their fingers together. Her hands were hot and sticky, and when Sister Ewostatewos looked down, she couldn't tell which fingers were hers.

"What are you afraid of?" Eris asked, for the third time, like Peter disowning Jesus before the sunrise. She had always believed that things asked in threes were great portents and here she was, calling down fortune.

She pressed their palms together and Sister Ewostatewos flinched. They matched again.

"They've found me," Eris said, so quietly that for a second Sister Ewostatewos thought she had only imagined this, her greatest fear made flesh. As far as she had gone, they were always bound together. That *me* meant *us.* Only the wall held her up. She thought she might—maybe she could—her brain reached for possibilities, but there were none.

~

Even in these most dire of times, the ordinary work had to go on. They could not throw up their hands and leave the ship to degrade beyond habitability, no matter what threat was waiting. Sister Ewostatewos still had to tend the plants, Mother Lucia still had to test the ship's nutrient levels and adjust its biochemistry. Sister Faustina still had to sit in front of her screens and filter through the messages that flowed into the array always and forever. It did not matter if today, just for a second but still a white-hot second, she hated the people who filled the vacuum with spam ads and useless data, nothing but nonsense that she was wasting so much time on. If she did not have a duty, she could just delete it all. She could just rip the wires from the ship's flesh and leave them to blissful, lonely silence.

Perhaps she could jump on a shuttle on the next station, go to the fourth system, still too far away to be more than a half-imagined frontier to the people waging a quiet war over the first three; take up farming on some isolated colony that needed bodies and wouldn't ask too many questions about where she came from as long as she could plant and hoe.

But she had never been a woman to take the easy way out.

Below all the dross, there were some messages to take heart in. One letter from Gemma to Mother Lucia, which

Sister Faustina forwarded to her tablet. Messages from a couple of stations and colonies, passing on garbled rumors about plague and conspiracy. None close enough to feel a threat, but too close all the same. A couple of the closest ones asked if they knew the convent who had developed a cure for the bloody curse of the universe. Those also went to Mother Lucia, so she could draft careful responses.

More concerning by far were the stranger rumors, of a murdered moon colony and an old woman who had died to stop it, all told with the singsong cadence of a homily. They were all a little different, all a little wrong in their timing and details, but too close to be anything but references to Phoyongsa III. One message she'd caught was a complaint about the students on St. Ofra, the only true university in this system, and how a faction of their students had become enthralled with some new anti-Earth revolutionary. *A cult,* the message had said, *though students often adopt extremes.*

And there was a message for her. Very short. *Dear Sister Faustina,* it said, *I have found good work raising the vegetables on a station near to Orion's Daughter. It is good work, though a lot harder on the body than the military. If you don't believe me, well, no one tells you when you join that the military is mostly waiting. If I do well at it my employer may pay for me to do a degree in botany on the planet. I think I would like that, should the world not end before it happens. Very best to you and yours.*

It did not need to be signed, though he'd signed it anyway. Sister Faustina didn't know why the soldier they had taken with them off Phoyongsa III had started writing to her—they had never agreed to it, and she so rarely managed to write back, not being much of a correspondent herself. Mother Lucia called him "her boy," as in, *I see there's another letter from your boy.* When she felt it was appropriate, Sister Faustina tried to offer him some advice—stay away from mining colonies that would have you be paid in company coin, never stay on a station where you can't figure out who owns it—but more often his messages were just like this, letting her know where he was. Once off the colony, he'd paid for passage on a ship with labor, and then spent some months building transponders on one of the big worlds close to the jumpgate to the second system. That, Sister Faustina had thought, was entirely too close to Central Governance, and he had evidently agreed. Orion's Daughter was a good planet to settle near. If he did well enough, perhaps he could get a place in the university there, get himself an education that did not require him to swear himself to an army or a church.

She had never wanted children of her own, was never interested in them beyond a vague warm wish for their well-being, but she found that she liked it when Mother Lucia asked, in passing, *Any word from your boy?* Yes, her boy, a man young enough to still find himself on a better path than the one he had been set upon. And that was what you wished for children, wasn't it? That they would find a better path than yours? She liked the thought of him elbow-deep in the coffee-dark soil that a successful farming colony cultivated, fragile root systems for soybeans or tomatoes or persimmons spreading out and out from where he planted them, the whole new world turning green. Someday, after he got the degree and if the world did not end. Such a strange phrase for them to have kept from Earth, *the* world, when so many spread across the sky, as many deeply strange as were familiar.

Though there was only one world now, when it was all on the edge of destruction.

Sister Faustina saved the letter into local storage on her tablet, as she had the others. She did not clear the record of it from the communications logs. She had nothing to hide; privacy was not in the life she had signed up for. But some things were, if not private, at least personal. How nice it must have been in the age when humanity was confined to only one world and you could send a letter on paper, with your own handwriting and your own fingerprints smudging the ink. She liked the idea of being able to keep her boy's letters in the pocket of her overdress, the weight of them always a reminder of him far away somewhere, growing new life on a world that had once been nothing more than a gaseous, methane-choked rock. Sending a letter like that now would be an astronomical expense. Each hand that passed it along would have to be paid or bribed in turn. The distance—and the odds that it would even find the recipient as they moved past each other in the wide systems—was astronomical. Even when Central Governance had held every known world and station and had claimed to have a standard mail service, people only sent paper by rare legal requirement.

There was a last message in the log, one Sister Faustina had avoided as she scanned through the list of advertisements and spam and inconsequential relays from their acquaintances. Another from Gemma, this time to her.

They had never been friends. Not even allies, really. Just two different people joined by happenstance on the same path. Gemma had never had that fervent belief, that shining trust in inner goodness that Mother Lucia had, but she held the same faith that Sister Faustina found incomprehensible. In her time in the order, she had met many women in this life. A few were like her, whose only belief was in the natural laws of physics and biology that they were forced to follow. Some were casual Aquinian theologists, who had laid the arguments out for themselves and decided that, on the whole, a belief in God was more logical than disbelief. Many lived somewhere on that pilgrimage from doubt to faith and back again, because for most faith was a constant journey, a choice to be committed to. And then there were those like Gemma and Mother Lucia, who seemed to simply *believe,* no matter how dark the world or how shaken their souls. Perhaps it was because they were both women of science. They'd simply woven the divine into their understanding of the natural order.

The hatches on the ship did not lock, of course. In the event of a hostile boarding, they did theoretically have the ability to flood the ship's hatch-sphincters with electricity and keep the muscles clenched, but even that was not the same as a metal door with lock and bar. She opened the letter.

I have spent some time considering what you've told me, Gemma wrote. No salutation. Well, that was fine. *It is concerning.*

Beneath the formality, Sister Faustina read her discomfort. She'd known she was asking Gemma to—do if not betray a confidence, then at least go behind a friend's back.

She hadn't known how to phrase her first letter. Gemma and her new crew were far beyond any ability to truly help—the last coordinates Sister Faustina had received for the *Cheng I Sao* set the ship near the jumpgate to the fourth system, and by now they were surely off in that strange and wild frontier. Yet she watched Mother Lucia wander the halls, saw her drifting gaze and her long silences, and it chilled something deep inside her. She had watched the former Reverend Mother's decline, after all. This was not the same, she knew that. Mother Lucia's body hadn't turned against her. The woman wasn't even thirty-five yet. But telomere degradation wasn't the only thing that could eat a person from the inside out. Finally, alone in the comms room sometime in the wee quiet hours after two bells, she'd chosen to begin with the same bluntness that usually served her: *Gemma—I trust you are well. I am writing about Lucia.*

Gemma's response continued: *I can try to write to her, but I'm not sure things are the same between us now. I have lost the authority to advise, now that I've left order and wimple behind.*

The correct response to that would be reassurance—of course you and Mother Lucia are still friends! Of course she still respects your counsel! But no, Gemma was right. There was a difference between being inside the religious life and outside of it. She had been one of them once, and she had chosen to leave, and no matter how much love lay between her and Mother Lucia, she could not bridge that divide now. Whatever she wrote to the mother superior directly would be set aside as the words of someone who had forgotten their duties.

I always thought of her as the only unshakeable one of us, Gemma continued, *but I suppose that this last year has shaken each and every one it touched. To ask her to continue as if we hadn't seen such horrors—as if we didn't have to look at all those dead people and know that God had allowed this—if she had continued just as before, don't you think we would be questioning if she had a soul, then?*

It was a good point, but beneath it Sister Faustina heard a protestation—surely this is only natural, and we should not be afraid? She sighed to herself. Optimism. Such a difficult thing to break through. She did not need reassurance that everything would be fine. This was a cold universe, and none of them could bet on that in the best of times. This was hardly the best of times. She needed Gemma to tell her how to reach Mother Lucia. They had been such good friends, surely there was something to say that would break through.

It's a lot of responsibility, Gemma wrote.

So is all of this life, Sister Faustina thought, uncharitably. *Perhaps all she needs is some time, and some quiet.*

The letter ended there, trailing off into uncertainty despite the lack of a question mark. Sister Faustina sat back in her chair. She thought about shooting off a furious reply—*Have you so thoroughly forsaken your sisters, that I would ask for help and you would refuse me?*—but no, Gemma had read her plea clearly enough. She simply did not have an answer. Maybe she wouldn't even if she had remained one of their number.

Sister Faustina checked the logs once more, but they revealed nothing new. Occasionally she hoped for a letter from Terret, the captain of that ill-fated colony the Sisters had rescued, and one of the too-few survivors. It never came. They had agreed to this, of course. They couldn't draw more connections between themselves and make it easier for Central Governance to track them down. Still, she liked to imagine the woman as second-in-command on a transport ship, perhaps, or head of operations on an agricultural world, with her husband and her baby in a small home with plenty of sunshine.

She stood up and stretched. Her lower back ached where the new ship's chair didn't have quite the support of the old one. This ship had been grown to their specifications, this chair supposedly coaxed into a shape based on the measurements of her exact body, and yet it would never be as comfortable as the one on the *Our Lady of Impossible Constellations*. Somewhere along their years together, her body had molded to it. Now she had a communications room that had been grown for her—she didn't even have to stretch to reach the manual controls now. The shipwrights had duly noted that the average height on a ship full of women would run slightly shorter than their default specifications and had adjusted all the geometry accordingly. It was truly an extraordinary art. Someday she would have to learn how they took a little gray grub and fed it and strung it through with wires and chemical supplements and made it habitable. For now, the new convenience of this ship offended her.

The world below the captured asteroid station seethed, roiling milky red clouds above a greening gray rock. Without a moon, the grand sea that blotted the western hemisphere lay still. Someday, Gemma imagined, it would be full of iron-rich kelp and fatty fish and everything else that would sustain the humans who were currently maintaining themselves on Argo Station. They were an intentional community; every resident paid into the terraforming project in equal shares. Very similar to Phoyongsa III, if an order of magnitude larger. She shook the thought out of her head. A brilliant storm crossed across the belt of the planet, bright with lightning.

"It's quite extraordinary," she said. "I've never seen a terraforming project this early before. Most of the good candidates in the other three systems have already been taken. How long will it be before you can live there?"

The man she'd just sold three tons of soy protein to waved his hand in a way she took to mean *sooner or later*. They were sitting in the station's community counter, something in between a bar, noodle shop, and distribution center. He shifted a little glass of something pale green over to her to seal the contract, and sucked down his own. "Two generations. My children's children will be the first adults who go down to build the settlement. If I'm lucky I might be sleeping on a warm sand shore in my dotage." He turned the glass over on the counter. Gemma copied him, though she hadn't gotten a taste for hard liquor yet and had to hide a grimace. "We're still selling community shares, you know. You and your crew could buy in. Cheap right now. We'd cut you in for even cheaper with a jump-capable ship like that, good trading I'm sure. Think about it, you and your wife's grandchildren could breathe brand-new air."

"Not my wife," Gemma said, though her stomach flipped. The alcohol, she told herself. Across the Argo's main hall, Vauca was making her own deal with two of the station's elders for some components for the *Cheng I Sao*'s communications array. She bent down to say something to the tiny old woman who clearly made the decisions, and the curve of her neck still made Gemma's heart still for a moment, despite everything.

The man chuckled. "Well, plenty of time for that before we go down."

Gemma smiled at him, but turned to the woman holding shift at the counter. "What's on offer today?"

"Sesame from the communal pot for a chit, hot broth and soy puff if you're paying in more."

Gemma opened her tablet and transferred the funds into the community's account, and the woman served her a steaming bowl with wheat noodles topped with tofu puffs stained red with chili and bobbing with flakes of white fish. Lots of fish in the fourth system. Tilapia could survive on worlds that weren't ready for humans yet, or be grown in the graywater tanks on stations. Cheap protein, especially when you were this far out from reliable mass manufacturing. She'd eaten a lot of fish this past year. She dipped in her spoon and drank it in. "Very good."

"Not much long-cooked food on an itinerant trading ship, I'm sure," her trading partner said. "Not a life many pick, no roots, spending most of your time with the same small crew . . ."

"I used to be a nun," Gemma said. "For a very long time."

The man leaned back in his chair. While the uncomfortable silence stretched on, Gemma fished the largest chunk of tofu out of her soup and said a silent thanks for the meal. Not a great deal of organized religion in the fourth system either. Plenty of gods, sure, but no one was quite certain how to deal with the existence of hierarchies and centralization. When she said nothing else, he grimaced and grabbed his tablet. "Well, good luck to *you* then certainly."

By the time Gemma had finished eating, Vauca had vanished. Back to the *Cheng I Sao,* no doubt. They had to leave dock here by eight bells if they wanted to get to their next buyers with time for their detour. Gemma shouldered her way through the crowd toward their bay. This was one of the first things she'd learned after she put away her old life and took up this one—even if she hadn't noticed it, as a sister in habit people had parted before her like the sea. Now she was just another trader in denim coveralls scraping by in the profit margin on soy protein and copper. When she caught sight of herself in the station windows it was like seeing someone with a face that was almost your friend's out of the corner of your eye. She wasn't old by anyone's standards, but she had entered the Order so young that she had had a different face. This woman with lightening brown hair and a smile line in the left corner of her mouth was a stranger. Her first month on the *Cheng I Sao,* she'd cut her hair off short in an inexplicable mood, and now it had grown long enough that the ends of it irritated her when it brushed the nape of her neck.

In the docking bay she typed in the code to unlock the hatch and let herself in. Jared was adding up their profit for the stop, and Gemma handed over her tablet to him. "I had some noodles, take it out of my share."

"Should've bought a book or a game or something too. At this rate you'll have enough to buy your own station soon enough."

"That's hardly true."

He tilted his head at her. She'd known it was a joke, but found herself unable to play the repartee. It was true, she had no idea what to spend money on. She liked good food when it was available. Otherwise she let it build up in the ship's accounting book. She'd tried to insist she didn't want a share at all, but Werrin had just shaken his head at her and added her name in the ledger. She turned away from the look. "Any letters for me?"

"None new. How are your friends? Have they saddled up the new ship yet?"

"Oh yes. I'm sure it's very nice. *Impossible Constellations* was and she wasn't even built for us. For them." Nothing more from Sister Faustina then, no more delicate phrasings that told her Mother Lucia was unraveling at the seams. Faustina had always been extremely pragmatic. Likely she'd written Gemma off as useless and wouldn't send another request for guidance. And she'd be right—Gemma was useless to them now. She had given up the habit and with it, any authority she had to comment on how Mother Lucia chose to lead her sisters. As close as they had been—nearly as close as blood sisters, oh, even though the Church said all religious sisters should be as close as that, it was rare to truly feel it—she'd lost the right to give counsel. Theirs was not a cloistered order, but there was the world and then there was *their* world, and the line between them as stark as any screen shielding the inside of a cloister. Yes, as well as she had known Lucia, Faustina could help her more than Gemma ever could now. "Let me know if more come."

"Of course I will." He wrinkled his nose again. Another small thing she'd said wrong. She found the idea of privacy and secrecy so strange here. A year on and she still wasn't sure what she was entitled to and what was the ship's business, or the captain's prerogative to keep secret. "Vauca's in the engine room. I think your little shiplings need a feed."

None of them were as subtle as they thought. Vauca could handle feeding their experiments on her own, but Gemma went anyway, so that the others wouldn't murmur around them quite so much. At least for today.

Their hypothesis that failed shiplings might be as valuable as their littermates capable of growing to habitable size was proving promising. Before they even met, Vauca had discovered that shiplings could live in barely shielded bubbles on the outside of a deadship and produce enough energy to cut fuel requirements by a quarter. Just as capable of photosynthesis and chemical secretion as full-grown ships. Now they were hoping these same shiplings in concert might be able to carry a deadship through one of the jumpgates that separated system from system. Space might be soft near the gates, but it was still incredibly costly for a deadship to accelerate through. Liveships might be less defensible and maneuverable than deadships, but running them was far cheaper.

Of course, their shiplings had to stop dying before they could really be called useful.

In Vauca's lab (*their* lab, Gemma reminded herself, she had outfitted half of it and poured her hours over the past year into her work here, no matter how much she still felt like a guest), the lights were turned low to avoid stressing the shiplings.

Vauca stood over the workbench with her oily coveralls half unzipped and the arms tied around her waist. In just a white undershirt, she was the picture of herself at their first meeting, and Gemma's heart fluttered again in a heady mixture of desire and nerves.

"Three more gone," Vauca said, and swept her hand over the soft gray bodies. The feeling in Gemma's chest cooled. The shipwright they'd bought this batch from had scoffed at their money. *They're not viable, you know. Damn things never last more than a few months if they don't develop. You're saving me the cost of recycling them.* Gemma crept next to her, keeping a few inches between them. Vauca shook up the vial with the liquid nutrients for the shiplings and hooked it up to the tubes that fed between the channels on the outside of the ship where the underdeveloped shiplings lived. At this stage, arrested before they could grow to even a hundredth of their final size, their brains were barely more complex than a guppy's. Vauca hypothesized that perhaps this was *why* they didn't grow—some quirk of the genetic engineering that created the species, an unfortunate genetic defect that afflicted most of their number.

Gemma stretched gloves over her hands. "Anything unusual about these ones?"

"You'll have to open them up to see for sure." Vauca had yet to look at her. The muscles in her back were as tight as the steel cables running across the ceiling above. Gemma felt the same in the tension in her jaw.

"I'm sure it'll be just the same as the others."

"Have to dissect them to know for sure."

"Yes, I know."

Vauca's hand clenched around the second vial and it slipped out of the intake. The ship rattled underneath them. Their business was done at the station. They had to lift off now if they wanted to have time for their detour. A month ago one of her biologist contacts from an exploratory ship at the edge of the settled universe had sent a letter about a story of a herd of rogue liveships around an uninhabited gas giant. Rogue ships—whose whole crew had died from disease or accident or attack, and had been left to wander alone—were rare enough. Liveships were too valuable to just set free outside the most extreme circumstances. The stories about them were mostly legend outside of a few accounts from the end of the war when there'd been so many vessels left derelict. To think some may have found each other and formed a herd? Extravagantly unlikely, but they were passing near the planet anyway. Gemma held the possibility up like an offering. "Do you think the rumors are true?"

Vauca's shoulders softened. The milky liquid in the second vial vanished into the intake valve. "If they were true, they may have moved on by now. But how extraordinary would it be! I've never seen one, have you?"

"Only once. I can't even say it was really a rogue ship the way most people mean. It was an extremist sect, sisters who believed that setting themselves out into the universe and letting the ship wander as it would while they prayed was the true way to follow God's will."

"How did they get supplies? Traders came to them?"

"I believe the thought was that God would direct the ship to land before the food ran out." She tried to shrug lightly, but the memory still gave her a shiver, even after all the worse things since. And they'd only been asked to come to help another abbey properly conduct last rites. "The ship seemed . . . confused. Though it was malnourished too. They're not meant to live on their own. I think we forget they're not wild animals."

"These rogue ships must be following some natural instincts."

"If we're not just chasing some old spacesick trader's tale."

The ship rumbled again and the gravity balance shifted. Gemma thought she could smell it when the deadship twisted its metal and plastic innards around to shift gears from orbit to planetside to space. It smelled vaguely chemical, like cleaning fluid. Vauca finished with the second vial, put it into the recycling bin, sanitized her hands. She leaned against the counter, leaving as much space between them in the small lab as was possible.

"Are you bunking with me tonight?"

Gemma's tongue stuck dryly in her mouth. She wanted to. She dreamt longing dreams in the spare bunk at the other end of the ship about letting herself into Vauca's room, slipping into bed beside her, the radiating warmth and soft rhythms of another body in the quiet, endless night. But she didn't know how to cross that threshold, no matter how much she wanted it.

Nothing changed in Vauca's face, but Gemma felt her mood shift from hope to disappointment. She nodded, untied the arms of her coveralls from around her waist and rezipped the top. "I'm going to install the new filters from the station—I'll see you at dinner." She went to move past Gemma, and Gemma's heart lurched. She made a noise she didn't mean to, and Vauca stopped. Gemma didn't know what she'd meant to say—what she even wanted to say, what she wanted at all—and instead she kissed Vauca on the cheek. There should be something more, she knew. She should know how to do this. But her hand hovered uselessly over Vauca's twill sleeve.

Vauca squeezed her hand, but dropped it. "Dinner," she said, and something strained in her voice before she left.

~

Sister Faustina counted the inventory as it came in. Most things they were able to trade for instead of paying hard currency, but they were still depleting their reserves. Once she'd broadcast their docking into the station's general news feed, they'd received one request for a mass and one to perform a marriage. That would bring in some small tithes. Though they would perform the services no matter what the petitioners could pay. Taking money for spiritual services always felt wrong, even if that was how churches and convents had sustained themselves for centuries. If they were lucky, they would have enough to eat meat once a week and keep the ship operating well within safety parameters. If they were unlucky, it would be beans, rice, and yellow caution lights for months. What they really needed was some colony with a whole crèche class ready for their First Communions.

Now there was a thought to make her feel a bit sullied.

Another set of footsteps came through the airlock. Sister Varvara, by the heavy sound of it. "Tell me you found a good price on the potatoes."

"He did take the beets for those. Also . . ."

"Also what?" Sister Faustina moved numbers back and forth on her tablet. She hadn't factored in carrots being so popular. They needed to change their planting.

"Also . . ."

"We don't have any more garlic; that was the last of it. Tell me you didn't promise any to the potato merchant." Sister Faustina looked up. Sister Varvara had the potatoes. She also had a young woman in coveralls.

"This is Kristen," Sister Varvara said. "She would like to formally request to become a postulant."

Sister Faustina looked at her careful calculations, the

hard mathematics of oxygen, water filtration, and calories laid out in percentages and decimals. They were calculated for exactly four women, not five.

Sister Varvara must have read her thoughts in the set of her mouth. "Mother Lucia should meet with her and give her petition the consideration it deserves."

"Of course." Sister Faustina stood up and laid the tablet aside. "Kristen, would you like to see our chapel? Perhaps you would like to pray before taking your petition to our Reverend Mother."

"Thank you, Sister," Kristen said. So formal. Suddenly she made a weird movement—the start of a bow, good Lord above, the girl was about to bow—before realizing that was silly and stopping herself short. "That would be lovely." Her fingers fluttered over her sides like the tiny butterfly-drones children these days played with.

Sister Faustina brought her back and sat her in the front pew and then closed the door to the chapel with a firm hand and went back to the cargo bay to discover exactly what Sister Varvara had been thinking.

Sister Varvara sat on the crate of dehydrated potato flakes, one clog-clad foot crossed over the other, as if she hadn't just thrown all their careful preparation to the solar winds. Sister Faustina drew herself up. "You should have turned her away."

"I did exactly as I should."

When Sister Faustina had first come aboard the *Our Lady of Impossible Constellations,* she had thought she might find a kindred spirit in Sister Varvara. They were both possessed of a certain sternness and sense of duty. But Sister Faustina had always been devoted to the idea of a purpose, and Sister Varvara, she quickly realized, was devoted truly to God, and a logical God at that. She was devoted to gospels and parables and papal decrees, and to the careful study and interpretation and implementation of such things. She strove to find a divine order in the universe and obey her place in that order. Sister Faustina thought the universe was mostly cold and random, a clock set and left by a distant maker, and strove to make it a little less cold.

"We aren't taking on postulants."

"And what *are* we doing?" Sister Varvara leaned back and the crate of potatoes groaned. "Do you know what we're doing? I do not. For months we've been flying moon to moon watching our backs, calling the time we spend hiding in the shadows of asteroids *quiet contemplation.*" She dropped her voice. "We have a cure for one of the most virulent diseases the universe has ever seen, we have significant evidence that Central Governance is trying to reignite a war that nearly ended us all before, and what are we doing, we are docked in this station doing two Masses a week as if that can be called a fulfillment of our spiritual duties."

"The Reverend Mother has been praying on it."

"The Reverend Mother is afraid."

"Of course she is!" Sister Faustina leapt to her feet and all the blood in her rushed hot to her head. "We are all afraid. I'm afraid, you're afraid!"

"And I still think we should not have gotten ourselves excommunicated if we did not intend on doing anything useful."

Sister Faustina sat back down. The tablet weighed heavily in her hands, these concrete reminders of their precarious existence. "I know."

The hatch sucked itself open again. Sister Faustina jumped. Mother Lucia turned down the corridor. She looked as she usually did lately. Drawn, worried, stretched taut like a fan belt before it snapped.

"We have a problem," she said. "There are issues with the ship's mechanical additions and many will need replacing. We'll have to reconsider our budget. Have either of you seen Sister Ewostatewos?"

"Mother," Sister Faustina began. She met Sister Varvara's eye. "There is a young woman waiting for you in the chapel. She wishes to join us as a postulant."

Mother Lucia shook her head.

"Why don't you speak with her, at least? Treat her petition with the solemnity it deserves."

Mother Lucia looked between the two of them. Sister Faustina willed her silently not to refuse. They might not need a postulant, but Sister Varvara was right, as much as Sister Faustina did not care to admit it. They did need a direction. They needed to do more than keep running from their own shadow. "All right. I'll speak with her. Please find Sister Ewostatewos and tell her to only purchase half the sodium supplements we'd planned on. We'll need to discuss the ship further when she returns."

She seemed like she might add something more—some further explanation of what was wrong with the ship perhaps—but then she shook her head and disappeared toward the chapel and the young woman who wished to postulate herself before God.

~

Mother Lucia sat in the chapel. She had been sitting in silence next to their girl for ten minutes, waiting. Waiting for what, she couldn't say. Divine inspiration. A miraculous lightning strike. Guidance, perhaps, but she had been waiting on that for nine months and it looked no closer to coming than it had when they parted ways with the *Cheng I Sao* on that small station. The girl waited silently beside her, hands in her lap. Together they stared up at the crucifix like it might take pity on them and break the silence.

Mother Lucia sighed. "Tell me, Kristen, why you wish to join our order."

"I've written a letter . . ."

"Tell me."

Kristen shifted in her seat. She didn't seem afraid. Mother Lucia knew afraid; this was just nerves. When Mother Lucia had decided she wanted to join the religious life, she had filled out an application and sent it along with a video essay responding to preset prompts. The process was different with every order and every system. Though it was really supposed to be more ordered than this. Were they still under the papacy, Kristen would have picked an order and been assigned to a house based on need; the choice to join their ship would not have been her own. The Order of St. Rita had convents on three moons, seven planets, and eight roaming ships like theirs spread across the four systems, along with contingents set to aid at several hospitals and tourist centers. On some corporatist colonies, they were the only healthcare offered. This was why it was a calling. You were not supposed to have your pick. It went against the nature of the thing.

"When I was little," Kristen said, "my father was a long-run ore hauler. He used to leave for months to take cobalt from our asteroid to all the stations and planets in the system. He wasn't really my father in the common-structure way of it. On my asteroid, we had crèches. Five or so of our mothers volunteered every few years to bear another set of us, and we were raised collectively. The cooperative board bought the seed for us from suppliers for the genetic diversity, so he was not even my father in that sense. But he was my first memory of a parent—I remember him lifting me off the floor and singing. When he was gone I used to sit in the viewing bay and use my astronomy coursebook to plot his path through the system, and I used to think, *let him come back.*" She stopped, and then touched her face lightly with the tips of her fingers like she expected to find something else in place of her lips and nose. "I'm sorry. That doesn't make any sense."

"I also grew up on an asteroid. When I was small, I used to lie awake and imagine I could hear the voice of God in the rovers working overhead."

"Yes! That's it. It's—the small things."

"Your father is all right with you taking this path?"

"He passed away."

"I'm very sorry."

Kristen turned to her. Her fingers were tangled up in her lap. Knots and braids. She was still as still could be. "He died of plague three years ago. He was working as a contractor for Central Governance. He came down with that kind of bronchitis they have in the second system. It might be a coincidence, but then, it also might not."

Mother Lucia took the girl's hand. It was cool, soft, dry. "We are women of the religious life, do you understand? We are not . . . revolutionaries. Or vengeance-takers."

Kristen smiled, a sad half-smile that tugged dejectedly at only one corner of her mouth. "It can be both, can't it? I have wanted to join the sisterhood since I was very young. Don't mistake me. I would have done so without his death, and without hearing about Phoyongsa IV. But Mother—it was revolutionary. Surely you know that. When I read the story of it, I thought, here is my small revolution, a revolution through the curing of the sick."

They had not cured many of the sick. Many of them still lay where they had fallen on Phoyongsa IV, their flesh returning slowly to the earth and their atoms to the churning pot of God's creation. Often, these days, Mother Lucia fell asleep counting their number to herself and reciting what she could of them. Alyse Martin, thirty-seven years of age, from Mars. Severn Jae, who made the rice they ate their first night on the moon, and who had a little scar like a fingernail across his eyebrow. She remembered every name. She always would. Every time one of the ever-changing rumors crossed their array she saw their faces again, and sometimes the faces of her sisters among them.

"How do you know about Phoyongsa IV?" When they left the last survivors on a station just outside the jump-point to the fourth system, Sister Faustina had insisted no one would learn of it. Mother Lucia had known that was absurd. But they'd tried their best.

"Coded channels." Kristen bit her lip, but evidently decided that if there was anyone to tell her secrets to, it was a nun. "They're out there if you know where to look. I'm a shipwright. My specialty is communications. Finding and decoding the hidden channels is a hobby."

"A shipwright?"

"Well, an apprentice. I was due to finish next year."

A shipwright, when they so badly needed one. Mother Lucia looked up at the bad carving over their altar. Although she was a faithful woman, she did not believe that people were simply fallen leaves to be swept along by the stream of fate. Sister Faustina would scoff and say there were many coincidences in this universe. She missed Gemma. They had shared a similar understanding of the world, balanced on a thin edge between fate and coincidence, human agency and a divine plan.

"I've heard about it," Kristen continued. "How ringeye swept the landing base. How they called for you not knowing if anyone was listening. How you came anyway, through the quarantine and the Central Governance ships, and sacrificed what you had yourselves to save them though there was no knowing it would work."

So it was one of the colonists telling the story, or perhaps Kristen had intercepted the chatter between the now-scattered survivors. Mother Lucia had not heard it from this angle before. This . . . heroic fable.

"Why do you want to join us?" she asked.

Kristen swallowed. "I would like to be a person who answers a call when no one else is listening."

She was a quiet and still young woman, as Mother Lucia had once been. If they were on Earth, they would not deny a request like this. There was plenty of room, and time, and spare water and air to let all postulants try the religious life. She was struck, suddenly, with a bone-deep desire to be able to speak with the old Reverend Mother and ask her advice. She had been—or so Mother Lucia had thought—one of the wisest people in the system. But of course, the Reverend Mother was dead. A martyr, practically, though of course she did not manage to martyr herself before all of them who relied on her learned that she had once been the figurehead of the government bent on bringing all the outer systems under the Earth's yoke. "We vote on things here. I can't just choose to take you on board."

Kristen softened against the back of the pew. Mother Lucia touched the back of her hand lightly. Let her have a little moment here before they returned to the others and asked for a vote. In her years of ministry, she had always found these quiet moments to be worth more than most prayers. The small pause, the space of a few breaths between a choice and making it, between one step and the next. A moment to stop and steel yourself or falter if you needed.

The door chimed. Kristen jumped.

Sister Faustina entered without waiting to be called.

"Sister—"

"You should come out here. Immediately." Sister Faustina pointed at Kristen. "Are we accepting her?"

"We'll have to put it to a vote."

"Then bring her too."

Mother Lucia strode out of the chapel. They were going to have words later, her and Sister Faustina. Some things were sacred. The ship certainly didn't seem to be depressurizing, so she couldn't imagine what was so important that they had to be interrupted.

For a split second, she had the terrifying worry that the ship *was* depressurizing, and all the safeguards and alarms had failed. She could imagine so clearly how it would feel. The swift wind that would suck all the air from her lungs. If she'd breathed in too recently, her lungs would pop like two bloody sparks. If she were too close to the breach, her body might be torn apart as she was dragged into the vacuum. Her breath stopped, her heart skittered like a startled bird. But no—she touched the wall of the ship and it was warm and alive and unharmed. Its heartbeat thrummed through its inner skin and the symbiotic moss covering it as surely as ever. She willed her own to match it. There was nothing wrong. Of course there wasn't.

She rounded the bend in the central chamber. She had forgotten Kristen behind her but now felt the young woman's eyes on her back.

Sister Ewostatewos stood awkwardly in the boundary between the docking ramp and the chamber like she was waiting to be invited inside. Then Mother Lucia saw the woman standing just behind, identical to Sister Ewostatewos in every way, down to the dark mole on her right cheek. Frighteningly identical.

The other woman stepped in front of Sister Ewostatewos. "Hello, Reverend Mother. My name is Eris, and I am requesting sanctuary on your ship."

Sister Ewostatewos's face twisted in a pained grimace. But she only met Mother Lucia's eyes and nodded.

"Well," Mother Lucia said, "we would never deny anyone sanctuary."

"I wasn't aware that you had a sister," said Sister Faustina, as blunt as a knife left to rust.

"I have many sisters." Sister Ewostatewos closed her eyes and tipped her head back ever so slightly, like she was searching for the heat from a sun. "All of you, every religious woman I have ever served with."

It wasn't an answer to the question that had been asked, and it hung in the air like a static charge.

Mother Lucia looked at Eris. "Why do you seek our sanctuary?"

Eris looked at Sister Ewostatewos. "I haven't done anything against your ethics."

"That isn't what I asked."

Eris licked her lips. She was fidgety woman. Was it from guilt? Fear? Just a natural tendency? Sister Ewostatewos stood behind her still as a reed waiting to be bent by the breeze. "Is it necessary to tell you why?"

"Oh, Eris," Sister Ewostatewos said. "Just tell them."

Eris just smiled, an uncomfortable thing without any teeth. "I do a lot of comms work now. I know exactly what you did on that moon, and that you're trying to hide it. I've run afoul of Central Governance too, doing some work for groups that aren't in their good graces. What better place to go than my sister's ship, when she's also trying to escape their long reach?"

That was barely an explanation. And precisely what they did not need—more trouble. But she had meant what she said. They didn't deny sanctuary. Not outright.

"Let's put them both to a vote," Sister Faustina said. "That's only fair."

"If we're to take on a postulant, what rules will we follow?" Sister Varvara asked, still sitting on the crate of potatoes. "When I first requested to join, I had to pay my first year's living expenses, but that is not the case for all abbeys. Will her postulancy be two years? Three? What if she makes it to simple vows—how long before we ask her to take solemn ones?"

"We will follow the standard path," Mother Lucia said. "Two years' postulancy, four years' novitiate."

"Then what of the vows? We can hardly ask her to swear obedience to the Church."

"Are we writing our own theology?" Sister Faustina asked. "It seems a dangerous path."

Mother Lucia cut them off. "If you are opposed to Kristen, say so now. The rest will need more consideration." Sister Varvara was right, of course. Too much of their procedure was based on being part of a network and a church they had now abandoned. They would need to confront that, and soon, before they began to run into the inevitable problems. They could not rely anymore on the security blanket of papal decrees and magisterium. Even distant as it was, the church had been a higher authority. Now they had no authority but their own.

No one opposed Kristen. They would have to work out the logistics now, but there would be plenty left for later—how they would go through the rites if none of them felt they could take confession, how long each stage would be.

"Gather your things tonight," Mother Lucia told her, as she herself had been told a lifetime ago. "We'll stay docked for two more days, and you're free to change your mind. No one will think less of you if you do."

Kristen nodded, but she didn't even look toward the loading bay and her old life. She would not be changing her mind. It was as she had said—there was no other order like theirs now, not in the whole of the four systems. They were, for better or worse, singular.

It was what it was. There were other matters to attend. "Speak now if you think we should refuse Eris sanctuary."

Sister Varvara's jaw worked. Sister Faustina looked down at the supply calculations in her hands. But they had never refused anyone in need. Never. They gave hospitality, and received whatever they were given in return. Some things, even under these most unusual of circumstances, could not be changed. Mother Lucia waited. The ship gurgled and shifted, and the recycling air hissed in and out of its inner pores. But no one raised their hand. Eris smiled, first at Sister Ewostatewos, who would not look back at her, and then at Mother Lucia. Mother Lucia returned the smile and felt it falter on her face. After everything they had been through, this moment should not be the one that felt like facing an oncoming storm.

Sister Faustina cleared her throat. "We also need to pick our next destination. No requests have come in for us."

"We could stay for a bit longer," Sister Varvara suggested.

"No," said Sister Ewostatewos, before Mother Lucia had to.

"I realize this is not what any of us wanted . . ." Sister Faustina looked at Kristen, and Mother Lucia saw her weighing the girl. "But what we've done is starting to spill over from rumors and hidden channels into the discourse. And there is something more concerning as well. Someone seems to be using it as—well, a rallying cry, I suppose. Or a prophecy. I'm hearing more and more about a group using the story as the foundation for some kind of holy revolution."

"A group?" Sister Varvara asked. Mother Lucia tried to keep what she was feeling off her face. She and Sister Faustina had talked about this already, of course, when the tales first started leaking across their feeds. A prophet, or a general, telling of how Central Governance was quietly killing whole colonies, how a nun had died to stop it, how they needed to rise up before it was too late. Most people they had encountered so far, if they'd heard of the group at all, seemed to think it propaganda for delusional youths. But that would not last forever.

"A cult," Sister Faustina said. "What's coming across

now sounds distinctly more religious."

"Who on the Earths would do that?" Sister Ewostate-wos asked. "Who'd expose all of us like that?"

"I don't know." That tension was right back behind Mother Lucia's eyes. "But it puts us in a difficult spot. There will come a point when Central Governance will want to put a stop to this."

"They have quite a following at the University of St. Ofra, apparently," Sister Faustina said. "Students always are good incubators for a revolutionary fervor. If the recent travel guides are to be believed, this leader is coming to the university shortly. And there's a genetics conference happening in a couple of weeks, around when we would make it there, with plenty of ships coming from all the systems, even from Old Earth. It's good cover for us. I say we go and at least try to understand what's happening."

"It's a Catholic university," Sister Ewostatewos added. "Well, technically. Maybe they would help us too. If we released our archives from Phoyongsa III, and St. Ofra backed us, it might pull the outer systems together."

"I don't like the idea of following this thing," Mother Lucia said. For all she knew, this cult could be a clever lure. Draw out the nuns with heresy.

"Don't you all have a story about walking into the lion's den?" Eris asked, from where she huddled in the shadow of a stack of supplies. Mother Lucia found her disconcertingly hard to read. Nothing showed on her face aside from a certain cool intelligence. "Perhaps it is better not to test whether your God will snatch you from their jaws."

"You're our guest, you don't have a say in this," Sister Ewostatewos said, with a thin, strained edge in her voice. Eris smiled at that, equally thinly, and leaned back against a crate of cell culture plates.

"We can't run from this forever," Sister Varvara said.

"She has a point," Sister Faustina said. "There will be Central Governance there. Scientists, for the conference, and they were invited, but . . ."

"Surely they wouldn't come for us on St. Ofra. It's the most populated, visible planet in this system. Hardly an anonymous colony ship that can be wiped off the map with no repercussions." Sister Varvara crossed her arms. "A conference like this is planned for months. It's not an elaborate ruse."

"That doesn't mean it isn't a convenient opportunity for them," Mother Lucia said. She could see it in her mind's eye—students caught in the crossfire, Central Governance implacable as they churned manicured lawns into mud and burned the library, her sisters hiding like mice until they were smoked out.

Kristen opened her mouth like she might say something, but then glanced at Eris and chose to say nothing. Smart girl. She was not yet one of theirs. Mother Lucia felt a small twinge of guilt for thinking that, but it was true. They were long past the point, all of them, where they could trust any stranger who came to their doorstep.

"Sooner or later, we will be caught. And what has this past year brought us? No closer to a decision, certainly." Sister Varvara jabbed a finger at the star map on the screen. "We have spent months doing what? Hoping this would magically go away? Even God is not that power-ful."

Sister Faustina sighed. "If we don't make a choice, someone else will eventually make one for us. And they have already—whoever is building this cult has decided to take our story and make it a weapon. We can't outrun this, Mother. It will sweep us away like a leaf on the cur-rent."

She was right. Mother Lucia was supposed to be lead-ing them, and so far what had she managed? A frantic flight from one backwater colony to another, watching their coffers empty and the rumors swirl anyway. "All right. St. Ofra. For their help."

~

The inside of the chapel glowed softly green. They had

turned off all the unnecessary chemlights and so were left with only the light that the ship produced as part of its biological processes. It turned the backs of Sister Ewostatewos's hands an inky blue when she gripped the squishy back of the pew in front of her, like she was the dark of space as seen through the soft-gaze filter of a planetary atmosphere. She let go and leaned back against the seat. The ship shivered—a small change in direction, a reaction to the solar winds shifting, something she would never even notice if she were working and not sitting in this silent room—and the biomass around her fluttered for a bare moment. Then the air in the room changed again, as the door sucked open and then again softly shut.

Sister Faustina stood next to the pew. She cocked her head at Sister Ewostatewos and everything that Sister Ewostatewos had prepared fled from her mind like a startled flock of starlings. And she had prepared an entire carefully phrased speech, the sort that would lead Sister Faustina slowly to the truth of what she was trying to say, so the shock would be blunted and the realization not as sudden as it could be.

"Won't you sit?" she said, and Sister Faustina obliged, folding herself into the narrow space next to Sister Ewostatewos. The ship's lights shifted to a yellower green and back again. A momentary spike in nutrients, or else a chemical imbalance she would need to check later. A good excuse to get up from here, put off the conversation. She made herself sit still. She took the hymn book out from the pocket in front of her. They had rescued the ones they could from the wreckage of the *Our Lady of Impossible Constellations*. This one was stained spine to fore-edge with the blood that pumped through the deepest arteries of ships like this, the same mineral color as brackish water. She flipped it open. The stain had spared most of the words except for "Lord of the Dance," where the beginning of the world through the Sabbath was lost to it, leaving just the last verses about the death and resurrection legible.

"I am supposed to be watching the comms," Sister Faustina said, with all the gentleness that she was capable of. Sister Ewostatewos sucked in a breath, but this was part of why she had asked her and not Mother Lucia or Sister Varvara. Sister Faustina would not sit here quietly with her and wait for her to be ready.

"Eris and I—" Sister Ewostatewos began, but all of it was gone. Her tongue lingered senseless on her lip, waiting for words to come. "—none of you have any idea."

"Whatever happened before you came to us," Sister Faustina said, "none of it matters. You know that."

"It does, now." Because she had brought this to their door. "My sister puts us in danger."

Sister Faustina sighed. "A propagandist for a minor

revolutionary cell is . . . annoying, to them, but it's hardly more danger than we put ourselves in."

"No, I—" She couldn't think of how to say it. "Eris thinks it's ridiculous that I'm here. She believes we're both damned."

"I haven't known your sister long, but she does not seem a person who I would trust on matters of damnation." If Sister Faustina was worried about offending her, she didn't show it, but she did add: "She seems to me a person who takes a lot of chances with herself, and in my experience, those people don't think very highly of themselves. Or others."

This was not untrue. Sometimes when they were younger and still together Sister Ewostatewos had thought that Eris clung so tightly to the idea of their damnation so that she had an excuse to dance on every tightrope she could find. Lifting pocket chemlights and nutrient supplements from shops in orbital stations run by cabals crueler than any sanctioned police force. Pushing their ships to the very limits of available fuel, threatening to strand them halfway between a derelict station and an unoccupied asteroid with no hope of rescue. When they had finally broken apart, in an unremarkable supply station in the second system, it had taken Sister Ewostatewos months to learn to live without her fingernails biting into the palms of her hands, to stop waiting for the next choice that would take them millimeters from death. And of course Eris had spent these last years working for ever more dangerous people.

"You know I came from the first system." This had been one of the first choices she made on her own. How close a story could she tell? How small a lie would hide her, how much of the truth was safe? "But I didn't come from a corp asteroid mine. We grew up near Venus."

Even out here, three systems and three jumps away, the adscreens and spam transmissions were full of sparkling pictures of the Venusian colonies. Bubble-stations like scattered jewels hanging in twos and threes through the yellowish sulfuric clouds, their transparent walls showing glimpses of the famous hanging gardens populated with engineered birds of paradise and beetles that were as pretty alive as they were delicious flash-fried and tossed in sesame oil. Venus, a paradise, where the system's best bioengineers went in the early days of settlement. During the war, many of those jewels had been shattered, and now lay dissolving on the acidic surface of the planet. But the clouds hid that destruction, and most of the bubble-stations had survived the war hiding deep in the cloud cover. Venus was a planet where you could forget the war, or at least that was what the advertisements sold in their glimmering, mid-millennium styling and slogans like VENUS: A CLASSIC GLAMOUR. Venus was a planet where you could pretend the past was nothing more than mild unpleasantness, that the four systems were all full of your choice of alcohol and your choice of drug and engineered playpets with golden fur to scoop away your litter.

Sister Ewostatewos had never known the Venus of the advids. She'd never even seen the bubble-cities gleaming like beads on a necklace or the poison-yellow clouds until the day when she and Eris had stolen a ship and escaped, and then she saw it only when she'd turned back for three seconds, long enough for Eris to shout at her that there was nothing to look back for.

She could still smell the inside of that ship if she thought hard enough. Sulfur, the stink of chemical cleaner, the sweet savoriness of burning meat and the sweat of the only man she had ever killed clinging to her hands like it would never come off.

"Not the bubble-habitats, I assume."

"No."

"I hear rumors once in a while on the comms. Military training camps scattered around the first system, children too young to be recruits. It did always seem strange to me that Old Earth had so few orphans for a planet so decimated only a generation ago."

Sister Faustina watched her, and Sister Ewostatewos was forced to nod.

"That is how most children get to the training crèche." The pew creaked under her as she shifted, not wanting to look Sister Faustina in the eye. "Eris and I were a little different. Our parents were rebels. Revolutionaries for a free Mars. Central Governance would probably call them terrorists, but they were more like flies trying to bring down a lion."

"I thought most of those kinds of cells died out shortly after the war."

"Yes, well, Central Governance keeps a tight hand on the news in the second system. Whether the planets there are technically independent or not." She bit her lip. Talking about this was always difficult. The memories smelled like burning rubber, sounded like half-remembered screaming. She wished she could puzzle together what had actually happened but it was all too far away, made of childish fantasies that had taken on the shine of memory and memories that had faded into fantasy. "I don't really remember much of this. We were very young. I've had to piece it together. But I think my parents' group downed an ECG supply ship. They were very quickly found and dealt with. Eris and I were deemed young enough to be salvage."

It came out before she meant it to. That was what each instructor had called them over the years. *Lucky to be salvage.* She could not even think of the rest, the brutal exams, the way the children had been set against each other, the ones who had not survived.

"And you escaped."

"We stole a shuttle." A tiny ship; it should have been too small to take them as far as it did. "We killed a man for it. Not a soldier. One of the mechanics." An innocent man, who had just as few options as they did.

Sister Faustina leaned back against the pew. Her confession hung between them. "And for taking a life your sister believes you're both damned. And you?"

"God grants forgiveness," Sister Ewostatewos said. "If you confess and repent. But I—" She had held this for years. Not a secret so much as a black mark inside her. "I've never felt sorry for it. I didn't *enjoy* it—though I think Eris may have—but I don't feel sorry. And I sit in this chapel every service and I wonder if that damns me in God's eyes."

Sister Faustina shook her head. "Far be it from me to imagine that I know the mind of the divine."

"That isn't very reassuring."

"If you wanted reassurance," Sister Faustina said, "you would have spoken to Mother Lucia."

She was right, of course.

"I cannot guess the mind of God." Sister Faustina suddenly, unexpectedly, laid her hand over Sister Ewostatewos's. The older woman's skin was cool and dry and she gripped Sister Ewostatewos's fingers in a vise. Sister Ewostatewos couldn't remember if she had ever touched

Sister Faustina before; it was as shocking as an apparition. "But I don't believe that the measure of a person is simply the number of good acts against bad. A person can hold both inside them. The Reverend Mother... none of us knows what to call her now. But know this—if I were the architect of Heaven, you are one of the first I would see through the gates."

Sister Ewostatewos pressed her other hand against her cheek and was both surprised and not to find the cool path of a tear there. She wiped it away with her thumb and Sister Faustina, politely, did not mention it. "I wish I could believe you, but ..."

"I understand. We simply do not get the answers to all of our questions in this life." Sister Faustina released her hand. "Now tell me, what is it you're afraid of?"

"My sister. Or what she might have brought with her." Sister Ewostatewos covered her mouth. She had tried for a long time to pretend she was a different person, that the habit had been a second baptism to wash away all that came before. But she never would be able to forget those years of following Eris across the systems, watching her hurt people to keep them alive and then, increasingly, just for fun. "I don't think she ... sees anyone but us two as real people. Or she doesn't care that they are. She just likes to break things, often enough. And she isn't telling me the whole truth. I know her well enough to know that. And anything else she is—my sister, my savior—she is also the person who scares me the most. Whatever she's hiding, it's bad. And probably dangerous."

~

Almost dinner, but Mother Lucia had enough time to check the comms array one last time before they arrived in St. Ofra's orbit. Sister Faustina, she hoped, would already be in the kitchen. She simply wanted a moment alone with the raw feeds, to check again that there were no traps waiting to be sprung, no massive Central Governance fleet or rumors of a new plague. Her head was too full of dependencies and contingencies to speak to anyone else right now. She hit the hatch button and the moss covering the ship's inner membranes split along its seams as the entrance opened. A pale face turned toward her, glowing in the chemlight-orange. Mother Lucia leapt out of her skin at the same time as the person said *Oh!* She cycled through the duty roster, but this room should be empty. And Kristen had no reason to be here at all.

Mother Lucia's stomach turned. "Why aren't you in your chamber?"

Kristen bobbed her head. Unsure or just wanting to hide her face, Mother Lucia couldn't tell. The comms screen was blank and empty. If she *had* intended to do something, she hadn't done it yet. "I was just curious about the system. It's my trade."

"Did Sister Faustina give you the passkey?" She wouldn't have, Mother Lucia knew, but this would be a very easy lie for Kristen to try, and therein admit she'd hacked their communications database. *Enough rope,* as the saying went, though as soon as the metaphor flashed through her mind the violence of it made her shiver.

Kristen paused—a second too long? Or was she only nervous? "No. I was only interested in the specs." She smiled in a way that Mother Lucia was sure she intended casually. "I've always liked the bits and bobs better than reading other people's mail."

"Sister Ewostatewos is serving lunch." Not that the girl needed informing; the twelve bells had chimed only moments ago. She touched the edge of the open hatch so the sphincter wouldn't close them in alone and waved Kristen ahead of her. "They'll be waiting for us to say grace."

"Of course." That head bob again. She looked like a little bird in the gray coverall and veil they had cobbled together for a postulant's habit—unusual for a postulant, but they'd agreed to grant her the protection of obvious devotion. She scanned the girl's face but whatever she was dreading or hoping for there didn't show itself.

When they reached the kitchen, Sister Ewostatewos was setting the last bowl on the table. Quick-heated radishes fresh from the hydroponics, the rest in a tub on the counter to be pickled or fermented for later. She sat as the two of them did. "Would you like to lead us in prayer, Mother?"

"Why don't you go ahead."

As she sat, she took stock of the sisters' moods: Sister Varvara watching Eris across the table; Sister Faustina, hungry, pretending not to watch the food steaming; and Kristen, perfectly serene at the other end of the table. Sister Ewostatewos said her prayer, though to her shame Mother Lucia did not hear the words as more than a sound moving over her, and after she filled her plate from the bowls that were passed without a care for what it was.

"Mother?"

"Hmm?"

Sister Faustina gave her that look, the one that made her feel like the other woman saw a countdown clock on her. Well, let Faustina do what she did and shuffle between them and all their secrets and faults. Today it must be Lucia's turn. "Kristen was telling us about her trade school, in the second system, one of the moons of Zenobia. Your station was near there?"

"Yes." A lifetime ago, when she was a silly little girl telling the rocks and the mining drones she loved them. "The asteroid's long been stripped, though; the station's abandoned now." She set down her fork. Perhaps she was being unfair to Kristen. She too had been overeager and clumsy once. "Though I never was on any of Zenobia's moons. Sister Varvara—you spent some time with the Paulines there, did you not?"

"Really?" Kristen blinked and there, again, that oddness, a tone not quite right. Nervousness, Mother Lucia told herself; she only wanted to impress them. "I didn't know that."

"I'm not sure how you would," Sister Varvara said. "I hadn't told you. It was only a season learning from their hagiographers. It was on the same moon as the trade school, actually. We ate in their canteen often and the students I think found us a novelty. What track did you do there?"

Kristen's face flickered. "Orbital."

Sister Varvara frowned. "Orbital? I thought they ended that track when I was there—before your time, it would have been. Maybe I have the wrong moon."

Kristen looked up, saw Mother Lucia watching, and just as quickly looked away.

"A lot of moons in the universe," Sister Faustina said. Surely she knew that they had to be on guard for every wrong thing; surely she saw this for the warning it was.

Mother Lucia slid her plate aside and pointed at Kristen. "Why were you in the comms room?"

"What?" Sister Faustina turned to her, and Mother Lucia held up her hand.

"Just now, she was in the comms room all alone, when she was supposed to be in prayer and contemplation. Why? And now we learn that she's lied to us about where she came from." Her mind worked—how much had they told her? Had she had enough access to their systems to download their archives, to plant a virus in the mechanical systems, or worse, a biological one in the ship itself?

"My own memory is hardly perfect," Sister Varvara said, even though, out of all of them, Mother Lucia would have expected her to hold a liar to account.

Sister Ewostatewos had paused with her knife halfway through a radish. "What is it you think she's done?"

Kristen's lip trembled, and that thing in Mother Lucia's chest that she had kept caged shook the bars. Kristen was hardly a child, and nothing yet had shown her to be the sort of woman who used tears as a weapon. "I don't know yet and I'd like her to tell us."

"I was only interested in the system," Kristen said. Her hands twisted on themselves. "I've only been on a liveship for minor repairs before—I wanted to understand it—"

"We were all entranced by the ship when first on it," Sister Faustina said.

"Explain the school," Mother Lucia said, and Sister Varvara opened her mouth again. "Not you."

Eris leaned forward, eyes glittering like missiles locking onto their targets, and Sister Ewostatewos shook her head at her.

"I don't know what you want me to say—"

"Mother—" Sister Faustina moved like she was going to take her hand. As if she was the former mother superior, dissolving into the foam of the past—well she was not. For so many reasons. She was trying to pull them back from the edge of a cliff, not leave them standing alone in the wreckage of her betrayal and sins. And Sister Faustina, of all of them—"Perhaps we should continue this with cooler heads."

"Enough!" She smacked the table and sent the cutlery skittering; the crack cut them all off. In the sudden vacuum, the ship's digestion sounded like a roar in her ears, or maybe it was just her own blood. Kristen's eyes shone. "What are you? ECG soldier? Someone sent from the Holy See to drag us back into line? An opportunist hoping for a bounty?"

Kristen started weeping. She made a choking hiccupping sound like a metal join someone had forgotten to lubricate.

"Perhaps—" Sister Ewostatewos began, but let the word die alone in the air.

"You're right," Kristen said. Sister Faustina's head snapped toward her. "I've been lying to you."

"You see?" Mother Lucia said. She tried to think of the closest stations that would let them leave someone. Before any of the others could respond, Kristen continued, "I thought you wouldn't take me if you knew the truth. I . . . would have deserved you refusing me."

"Well, you had best tell us now," Sister Varvara said.

The girl sniffed and sat up a little straighter, gathering herself. "I didn't have many options when my colony dissolved. My father was dead, and while all the adults were our parents, no one else really laid claim to me. I was eighteen then, and there were plenty of younger ones who needed looking after." She wiped her cheek with her sleeve. In the bluish glow of the chemlights she did look very young. "Central Governance was recruiting on the mining platform where we split up. They wanted peacekeepers, they said. Only within the jurisdictions of their few stations. I have always been very good with communication systems and relay structures, and they said I could go into that after a few years. I just had to do a stint with the peacekeepers first." Sister Faustina grimaced and rubbed the spot where her wimple met her forehead.

"And you did something for them you regret," Sister Varvara said, with a heavy weight on the *something*.

"Not the way you think." Kristen lifted her hand, gesturing to one of those feelings that could never be encompassed in words. "I never hurt anyone. I was only in for a year, and they only let me off the base once. Me and three others went to repossess a colony ship the family had taken an ECG loan for. They got scammed on the land grant, didn't have a thing left to their name. Three little kids who thought they'd finally see an atmosphere after years of asteroid life." She ducked her head away from all of them. "I just felt . . . dirty. We docked at a station where we were ordered to maroon them and I just . . . walked away."

"You're a deserter?" Sister Ewostatewos asked. Her sister made a face that Mother Lucia couldn't read.

"I thought—after what happened to you—you wouldn't want anyone who had even brushed up against Central Governance. But coming here felt like the *right* thing."

Silence fell over the table; it felt like the ship itself was holding its breath. They all jumped when Sister Varvara drove her fork into a carrot with a crack. Sister Faustina cleared her throat. "You should have told us the truth. Many of us didn't come here along a perfect path."

Kristen looked to Mother Lucia, the picture of penance and penitence. Sister Ewostatewos patted the girl's shoulder gently. Mother Lucia looked to the others—Sisters Varvara and Faustina, they had always understood necessity. "We should let her off at the next station." Kristen froze. "At a minimum, we cannot trust anything she says now, and having a deserter only brings more risk. At worst, this is a convenient lie covering a worse one."

"Let's take some time before we make any decisions," Sister Faustina said.

As if she didn't know how much danger they were in already, every day, and how difficult it was for Mother Lucia to try and steer them from it. "What time do we need? Honesty is part of the process of postulancy, and she's broken that already."

"We all have a past," Sister Ewostatewos said, and Mother Lucia didn't like the glance she exchanged with her sister. Many of them had elided their pasts, it seemed. Mother Lucia wanted to scream. Perhaps she alone had started this path by offering up her whole heart.

"No, I understand." Kristen's voice wobbled. "You have no reason to trust me. I just—I was ashamed of it. But I shouldn't have lied. I did write the truth in the confession book though. I would not have betrayed that. You can—I really *would* understand if you ask me to leave."

"No, no, wait," Sister Faustina said. "We do things by vote here."

"Do we even need to vote?" Mother Lucia already had the path in her head. It wouldn't burn too much extra fuel to detour to an iridium mining operation nearby.

"I lied to a priest to get here when I told him I had the

faith. I don't think this is a mortal sin."

Mother Lucia looked at them all and for once felt like she could not tell what a single one of her sisters believed. "Fine, then. I vote she goes."

"I vote she stays. For now." Sister Faustina met her evenly.

"Stays," Sister Ewostatewos said.

Sister Varvara chewed a cold carrot while she mulled. She had argued for equipping this ship with offensive weapons systems, though the rest of them had disagreed; surely she would see the risk. "I vote she stays. To base our community on perfection—which of us would live up to that?"

"Have you all forgotten this past year?" She couldn't believe it—all the careful checking of station docking logs, lest they land at the same one as an ECG ship; the bare margins of food and fuel now that they had lost their maintenance funds from the Holy See; the nightmares where she woke up cold and more alone than she had ever felt in her own ship before. She stood up too fast and her chair thudded into the wall behind her, and the moss turned a sudden, stung green. Her sisters stared at her. Everything she wanted to say was a thing she would have to ask forgiveness for later if she let it leave her lips. So she did not, and only turned and left.

In the chapel she knelt on the floor and closed her eyes

and tried to ask God to show her again that love she had once held for every imperfect thing, that had sustained her through so much. Instead she only felt that same cold fear that they were walking a path toward destruction and there was nothing she could do to turn them from it.

~

Sister Varvara found the girl in her chambers later, after they had swept the remains of the ruinous meal away, folded over a psalm book closed in her lap. She suspected that she didn't believe she'd be allowed on other parts of the ship, which was certainly not the worst assumption to make. Sister Varvara appreciated a person with healthy caution.

"I'm sorry," Kristen said, when she jumped at the older woman's entrance. She lifted the book. "I was . . ."

"Praying?"

"I suppose. Wishing, maybe."

"Much the same thing." She gestured to the side of the bed. "May I?"

Kristen moved over.

Sister Varvara sat and took out her tablet. "It's unfortunate you've walked into a situation you know only half of."

"I'm sorry—"

"I don't need your apologies. But I think you should understand." Sister Varvara searched for the right words. She had always found faith to be a sturdy and useful object. A central beam in the construction of the universe, perhaps, holding up the structure. A constant but not one she was always aware of. It was difficult to describe how, after Phoyongsa III, it had seemed like the ceiling might come down. "I suspect you came here as much because of the rumors about our actions as you did to dedicate yourself to worship." She didn't wait for Kristen to argue. "You must understand that we aren't revolutionaries here. We help where it is needed. I am afraid none of us are eager to be holy martyrs, not when we can do better work alive. And what happened on that moon . . . I imagine the stories are significantly less bloody and more heroic."

She turned the tablet on, and opened the recordings that she had selected. The cameras on their vacsuits were shaky, the microphones even worse, but they showed it well enough. She did not want to watch it play out again herself, so she watched Kristen's face. Nausea at the state of the bodies, horror at the marines so eager to harvest misery, and then their own wails when they realized their ship and abbess were dying above. At the end, the girl was shivering.

Kristen licked her lips, shook her head. Her mouth

opened and closed wordlessly. "I didn't know it was like that. So . . . brutal."

"The worst to me is the waste of lives," Sister Varvara said. "Potentials. The powers on Old Earth find life very cheap, and that disturbs me. To Mother Lucia, I think the worst was how it ended a certain belief she had, that the universe arced toward goodness on its own and that all things had a purpose. And now we have asked her to lead us, to define our purpose and our path."

"I see," Kristen said. She touched the screen, frozen on footage from Mother Lucia's camera. Terret covered in blood, with her chest heaving for air, her expression desperate.

"I hope so. We aim for generosity, but after that moon, none of us has the open heart we once did. The whole foundation of our world crumbled. I think there are very few people in this life who understand what it's like to bind your whole life not to a family, or a career, but a *devotion*. To be betrayed by the Church, to see it murder and twist the trappings of holiness for mortal ends, it feels almost like being betrayed by—" She could not quite bring herself to say *by God*. But the look on the girl's face said she had finished the sentence for herself. If she was to be one of them, she'd have to understand this wound and the scar it left. She tapped the tablet. "I'll leave this with you for a bit, in case you need to look again."

~

"You know what anyone else would call a person who has heard God's voice." Mother Lucia paused. Sister Faustina stayed quiet. There were things they had to discuss—concrete, necessary things, like how the ship was still low in iron and there was nowhere to trade for supplements within the next week's travel (not that they had the spare funds for concentrated supplements in any case) so they would need to find another way to balance the levels. "What you and I would call such a person, had we heard the story from the Church's archives or in liturgical studies. A person worthy, for a moment, of that highest grace."

"You might say such a thing, perhaps," Sister Faustina said. Mother Lucia looked at her from under the edge of her wimple, shoulders bowed inward, rosary tangled up around the fingers of her right hand. They had gotten this rosary, along with six more identical to it, at the station where they'd waited months for their new ship to grow to spaceworthiness. It wasn't artful. As best Sister Faustina knew, it was just a salable way to deal with the junk left from deadship repairs. Other stations might smelt it down and make chess sets or belt buckles; this one had just found that rosaries left the shelves fastest in their small corner of this small system. At the time, it had seemed necessary that they replace all the material accoutrements of religion that were lost with the *Our Lady of Impossible Constellations*. Now, Sister Faustina looked at the rosary and saw enough money to cover another week of rice. "I am of course the practical sort."

It was intended as a joke, and a joke at her own expense at that, but Mother Lucia frowned.

Once and not so long ago, Sister Faustina would have called Mother Lucia a friend. Someone whose mood she could anticipate and who she could understand with a look. Now, she felt the way she often had as a child—awkward, perpetually too blunt, stumbling ungainly through unfamiliar terrain.

"I did not hear the voice of God," Sister Faustina said.

"Didn't you?" Mother Lucia asked. "Is it necessary for God to speak to you in human words?"

Mother Lucia was the only person Sister Faustina had told about her experience on Phoyongsa III, when they were both trembling and flecked with smoke and blood in the storage bay of the *Cheng I Sao*. She had barely known how to explain it. The farther they got from that forsaken moon, the less it seemed like a real memory and the more like something she had dreamed up in the aftermath to make sense of why she was not dead, though she knew from the timestamps on her own logs that she hadn't slept before recording it. Now she had trouble even describing what had happened without going back to those logs. She had been standing in the plague colony, surrounded by the dead, in front of a boy who wanted nothing more in that moment than to kill her. And then, the air—or the light, or both—had changed, had become for the smallest second some other kind of force, and he had chosen the world where they both lived.

Mother Lucia was right. This did sound like the sort of thing a saint would say. She saw the other woman's hands clench.

"I have no desire to be a saint," she said, as much to Mother Lucia as to anyone else who might be listening on this plane of existence or another.

"That's a very pious thing to say," Mother Lucia replied, and now it almost had the tone of a joke.

"It's not for any pious reason. I've read all the hagiographies you have. You know how they end. I would prefer not to be burned at the stake, or beheaded, or buried alive."

"What would you prefer? If you had to choose an end."

What a question. She couldn't even contemplate the answer. A small prefab on a colony just finding its legs, an old woman who could be trusted to provide the right medicine and the right advice, until they found her dead in the night one cool morning when the face of the planet had leaned away from its star? A chamber much like the one she had spent the past years in, taken in the transit between two systems, a person one moment and gone from this earthly form the next? She had never been good at imagining the future, not beyond the next step. When she was young, she had thought this was what had saved her from the mines—she had not been able to think far enough ahead to be paralyzed by indecision, only enough to seize the choice that seemed like it would most immediately take her away from that hellish place. Now she wished she could contemplate what it might be like to be old, to see the ripples of the choices available to her. "Something quiet, I think." She coughed—something dry in the air today, maybe because of the missing nutrients in the ship's system, maybe some bug she had picked up on the station—and held out the tablet to Mother Lucia.

The numbers were self-explanatory.

"I don't like that there are Central Governance ships here," Mother Lucia said. "Even if they're theoretically invited to the conference." Also self-explanatory. The number was not so high as to be immediately alarming. At least not to any of the surrounding planets and stations. Coincidence could be merely that. What seemed like a threat could be just their terrified brains jumping at shadows and possible hunting parties spelled out in ship signatures on their dashboards. Space had a way of making ghosts. Sister Faustina had met enough old traders hunched over moonshine in dark corners of desolate stations, one hand always on a weapon because they saw every human as a threat.

"It would be a mistake to think they just let us go." She phrased it carefully. Their old ship had been destroyed, there was no way for Central Governance to know the signature of the new one yet. But there were also not so many groups of nuns traveling this system that they could hide behind the others. They were not anonymous. The question was whether they were trouble enough to be hunted down. And then there was the matter of Eris—nervous, strange, hiding something. And the impression she made on Sister Ewostatewos, who had been sturdy as a rock, the most of all of them, until her sister had emerged from out of the black. Whatever the twin had gotten herself mixed up in, Sister Faustina would not be surprised to find that it had Central Governance at the end of it. All roads lead to Rome, all trouble led back to Earth and its keepers.

"They are making sure we mind ourselves. If we do nothing to provoke them, they won't harm us. They wouldn't want the spectacle of it." Mother Lucia grimaced as she said it. Sister Faustina knew the feeling exactly. They were ants hoping the elephant would not care enough about their annoyance to step on them.

"Don't we have a duty to do more than save our-selves?" Sister Faustina asked. The obvious question. There was war blooming like a night frost right beyond the horizon. War, and death, and sickness like these newest systems had never seen, not even in the great decimation of forty years past. These past few months, deep in their sleep cycle, she sometimes heard frantic murmurings on the other side of Mother Lucia's cham-ber door. She knew those dreams herself, fever-pitched prophecies of a war-torn future to rhyme with the bloody past.

"I also do not wish to die a terrible death."

Sister Faustina tried to smile, and felt it slip on her face, poorly fitted. "You don't desire sainthood?" The joke wasn't even funny to her own ears this time.

"We are a handful of women living in a small bubble of air. What would you have us do?"

She did not know. "I think this is when I should re-mind you of the story of David and Goliath."

"David and Goliath? We aren't David, we're—a speck of dust in Goliath's eye."

"The story of Phoyongsa III will come out. It's al-ready starting. Either we can tell it or it can be told for us." She did not tell Mother Lucia about the most dis-turbing thing she had seen come through the comms array today, the thing that had first come to mind when the mother had brought up sainthood. She had gone digging for it, in the hidden, mostly illegal data packets that were traded at stations like this. She had needed to know what they were saying. Already there were five or six incomplete versions of the story circling. In one of them, though, there was the line, *she gave her life for them.* As if the last Reverend Mother had been nothing more complicated than a pure-hearted old nun. The way it was written—that reverence—Sister Faustina had closed the text file and had not yet been able to bring herself to read the rest. "If we do not act, the path will be chosen for us, and we may not like where it leads."

Mother Lucia closed her eyes. The ship shivered—a cough, or just a small muscle spasm, a barely noticeable temperature change in the life support systems.

"Someone is telling the story," Sister Faustina said. "We can choose to be a part of the telling or not. I would say not, if I thought we could escape the reach of it. But short of leaving this system and hiding in the dead moons and water worlds in the fourth system, I do not believe we can. So we should try to make sure we like the story."

"I thought we had an agreement. We go our separate ways, bury the story, keep everyone safe."

Sister Faustina said nothing for a moment. She knew

they were thinking of the same thing—a dead ship, floating torn and bleeding over a dead moon, belly full of its
dead babies and a dead woman's body. Their lives had always been fragile, governed by cold calculations and the
precious needs of water and air and chemical reactions.
But they had managed to forget that. Now they were
alone, possibly hunted, and deeply, constantly aware of
how easily they could be shredded through on the whims
of an implacable many-headed hydra that thought of
nothing but power and hunger.

"It was naive of us," Sister Faustina said.

Mother Lucia tilted her head back until the edge of the
back of the pew cradled her skull. "How appropriate, as I
do feel so very naive."

"I've sent word down to the university," Sister Faustina
said. "One of the trustees will meet with us tomorrow. I
get the impression they are already well aware of what we
wish to discuss. Sister Varvara and I could—"

"No," Mother Lucia said. "You and I will go tomorrow."

~

The trustee who met them in the office was a tall, pale
man who had cultivated for himself the look of a classical
Spaniard out of Terran historical dramas even though

he was at least a century away from his Spanish forefathers and they were all many centuries out from the last of the matadors. Mother Lucia thought there might be something different about the gravity in this office—a slight increase, barely edging into what was consciously noticeable—to make the broadcloth swing so dramatically around him. What waste. This planet had an amiable gravity already. There was no need to spend the resources on generators.

The trustee gestured to the two seats on the opposite side of his desk. Mother Lucia had been to the University of St. Ofra once before, a stop midway between the asteroid mining operation where she'd grown up and the moon in the second system where she had started her novitiate. She'd taken in only a few things. The long curving walkways inside the habitat-bubble, meant to evoke the meandering, many-layered architecture of al-Qarawiyyin and Oxford. All the students, more people than she had ever seen in open air in her life, who giggled and chattered amongst themselves and paid no attention at all to the young woman in modest clothing. And plants, so many plants, some that weren't even edible or medicinal but were grown for purely selfish aesthetic purposes. She had touched a rose next to the bench where she waited for her next shuttle, pricked herself, and led the blood drip back to the soil. A small card under the bloom informed her that this varietal had been brought all the way from Old Earth, and in the distant past, had been the prizewinning favorite of the princess of a kingdom that no longer existed.

Now she settled herself into one of the large chairs and chose to tell herself that this distinctive woodgrain had been produced to spec somewhere in the system, and not shipped all the way from the first at what would have been a truly ludicrous waste of resources. The trustee set himself down on the other side of the desk. Sister Faustina stood a second longer, looking down at him with an expression that Mother Lucia knew at this point to be distaste, and then she too sat.

"Sisters," he said, warmly. Mother Lucia's neck prickled. She had, as she was sure Sister Faustina would say once they'd left this room, the distinct sense that this man was going to try to sell them something. "Could I offer you some tea? We grow the real thing here in our Botany department."

"No, thank you." She wanted tea—the air in this room was too chilly, probably to discourage complaining students and faculty from staying too long—but often it paid to play into people's image of the ascetic, self-denying religious. It made them think you otherworldly and ascendant.

She did not like how this calculus now played out in her head. Was this how her predecessor had felt? No decision ever made out of pure faith, just the endless mathematics of manipulation and conflicting motivations.

Your predecessor was a war criminal in hiding, she reminded herself. She and Sister Faustina had never spoken of this after they returned from Phoyongsa III but she knew—hoped—that they were kept up at night by the same uncomfortable thoughts. Had they been led for years by a woman motivated by nothing but a need to hide? Or had the Reverend Mother truly believed? Could belief redeem someone who had so nearly ended worlds upon worlds? Mother Lucia believed in forgiveness, she truly did believe that anyone could pay their penance and be forgiven in the eyes of God, and had anyone else asked her she would have said that there was no soul beyond redemption. But heavenly forgiveness was a different thing from forgiveness in this life. And Mother Lucia was finding that she had a hard time forgiving deception.

"We've come to you because St. Ofra has always been the center of the third system," Sister Faustina said, and Mother Lucia realized she had been quiet a moment too long. This was a pleasant untruth. Many would call St. Ofra the center of the system, but just as many would name the shipyards on the Moons of Herold or the jumpgate, the soft spot in space that connected this system to the other three and all the stations and ships that had grown up around it like barnacles. "You have always believed that the third system could mean just as much for humanity as a whole as the first system does."

"It's why the university was formed," the trustee agreed. He had told them his name, though it had slipped out of Mother Lucia's mind seconds after it had slipped out of his mouth. Something bland that she had to suspect was as much a production as his dramatic clothing and polished boots. Dominguez? Yes. Mr. Dominguez. It was a tell that he had asked them to use the English honorific instead of the Spanish. "How unhealthy a world it would be where we were all dependent on Old Earth for our great art, our grand music, the best education, and cultural exchange? Yes, we would all be much the worse for it. Central Governance wouldn't need weapons, we would all just bow to them."

"Then you must understand the threat."

"I've heard the rumors. Plenty spreading among our students—especially this . . . *club* or whatever it is. Ringeye, a weapon of Central Governance? Disturbing. Disgusting."

"We are only a few women, there's little enough to back up our story. If St. Ofra verifies our claims and supports us, we have a chance of uniting the outside systems."

Mr. Dominguez laughed. "What a dream that is. We've been talking about a coalition to equal Central Governance since my grandfather was a boy and the fourth system was nothing but a handful of mining operations and unexplored dirt."

"Your students find it a worthy cause," Sister Faustina said, and the corner of Mr. Dominguez's mouth twitched, but he only said, "A big dream for those with big long lives ahead of them. I am sure when the both of you were university students you dreamed a great many dreams indeed."

Neither of them had gone to university. Sister Faustina had gone straight from her colony to her novitiate. Mother Lucia had trained as a doctor not at a university, but at a hospital. The spaces were simply too vast here, the need for doctors too great, to rely on the old system of putting students through a few universities and then shuttling them off to residencies and shuttling them back again to the positions they were awarded. Hospitals out here simply set up a few classrooms, advertised the specialties they were needing, and built instruction out of a mixture of their own staff and virtual education.

"I never had the pleasure," Sister Faustina said, with that cutting edge she used to remind men like this that most of the lives in this system—most of the lives across all four systems—did not come with imported zebra-wood chairs and extravagant, useless foliage.

Mr. Dominguez took it not as the rebuke it was, but as a reminder that they were religious sisters. "Of course. My apologies. I am not actually familiar with your training. Although St. Ofra does have a Catholic history, we moved in a more secular direction many years ago."

This man would keep them in this office all day making circular, meaningless pleasantries. Mother Lucia straightened her back and he seemed to really notice her for the first time. That was one thing she wished she had taken the time to learn from her predecessor—how to command an aura of authority. Or maybe that was the sort of thing that only came with practice. Or with being a war criminal. It must have taken a lot of a certain kind of steel to stand in front of a microphone and ask hundreds of worlds to turn on each other just for the sound of your beloved voice.

Stop it, she thought. "Let us get to the point, Mr. Dominguez. I'm sure you have other appointments in your calendar today. Will you help us? St. Ofra could truly be the center of the third system. If you stand behind us, and call the rest of the worlds to you."

He sighed, twined his fingers together, and cupped the back of his head with them like this conversation had been so truly exhausting. She knew then, that they would be left alone for the wolves. "We have a certain responsibility to our students. The university cannot undertake any action that would endanger their safety."

"Your students will do as they like whether or not you support them."

"As is only to be expected."

"And many of your donors are very conservative with their money," Sister Faustina said. She drummed her fingers on the glass-top table. It sounded like rain, another half-remembered sound that Mother Lucia had not heard for years. "You have an endowment to think of."

"We do." He softened. The neatly trimmed beard, the great cloak, the nice shoes all looked on him now like a costume that fit poorly, and Mother Lucia felt that she was seeing for the first time in this tedious meeting. "And Central Governance supports us too. Not with direct funds—I am sure you never would have come to us had that been the case—but by sending us books and scholars, supporting exchange, funding the infrastructure that keeps us connected. They still own so much of the universe. And the truth is that our funding has never been the same since the war. Our founders could live as if this world were a kingdom unto itself, self-sustaining and independent, because they had enough money to purchase that independence and they lived in a time when much more was freely given. We, simply, do not. Despise me if you must. I know Central Governance would have us all on their work contracts again if they could. I'm not blind to it. But imagine what happens if we throw in with your lot and you lose, as you know you almost certainly will. St. Ofra has the only press in the outer three systems that has sustained publication for more than twenty years at a time. We have the only genetics program that could even hope to match, someday, the work being done in ECG labs before the war. One of our researchers is *this close* to discovering how to increase the viable yield of a litter of shiplings tenfold. Imagine a universe without us, Sisters."

"The university system is hardly necessary to human advancement."

He shrugged. "Perhaps not. But we have certainly accelerated the advancement of these newer systems. None of us are children, surely. We all have considerations beyond the great noble purpose. I do not want to risk the destruction of the university or the lives of our students; I also will not risk our operating budget. The board has already come to their conclusion. You are welcome to any of the publicly accessible resources St. Ofra can offer, like any other visitor. Rest your ship, take part in the communal meals, spend some time in our libraries. But we will not aid you beyond that."

He stood, and that was their cue. Sister Faustina's cheeks were pink, but Mother Lucia felt only a cold flush, like she had stepped into a lake in winter and was now looking up as she sank, looking toward a gray and dying light.

Did the board of trustees know that they had just issued a likely death sentence? Did they consider it a reasonable sacrifice?

Outside the office, they stood under a banner that proclaimed THIRTY-FIFTH INTERWORLD CONFERENCE ON THE STUDY OF HUMAN GENETICS amidst sleep-deprived researchers from a bundle of worlds. The scientists swept around them, too intent on getting to their next paper presentation to pay any attention to the two women in black. Another group of students—dressed mostly in the yellow color that had become a kind of outer system badge, given how it looked like the crackle of energy across a jumpgate—held signs with slogans like EARTH STAYS ON EARTH. The protesters did not make the connection between these two nuns and the order who had released the true story of ringeye. Mother Lucia watched them and wondered how many of them would sign up to stand in another rebellion. She had not been alive for the first one, and her own lucky parents had lived too far on the frontier of the third system to see more than a skirmish in their planetary system. But plenty of the miners who had signed work contracts while she was a child had come bearing stories of how they had learned to lay explosives or wear a vacsuit in the war. Forty years. Enough time for the worst of the pain to be forgotten.

Sister Faustina eyed the protesters and Mother Lucia knew exactly what she was thinking. They could hand this group their files, everything they had learned on Phoyongsa III and everything Eris and Sister Ewostatewos had revealed. St. Ofra would have united the outer systems through the force of influence and legitimacy, but a grassroots discontent could bring rise to the same thing.

Or it could bring all the worlds squabbling amongst themselves, some withdrawing into paranoia and xenophobia like that would protect them, others hurling themselves against the might of Old Earth in the belief that making the first strike was a winning gambit. She remembered some of the recordings Eris had showed them, the ones smuggled off Earth despite the commsnet. President Shen speaking carefully into a microphone, lightly, like he was just making a joke. *They think they can live without us,* he said, and the crowd laughed. She always wondered about the crowd—had these recordings been made in a stadium? A studio with sycophants hand-selected for their warm and convincing laughter? Or was it just a semblance of a human noise created by a looping computer program? *They think they can live without us, when it was our wealth that allowed their existence at all, our knowledge and resources and willingness to shepherd those colonies through their first trembling steps. You few who have family in the outer systems—do they not still wait on pins and needles for the next episode of the hottest Mars audiodrama? Do they not relay messages to you through the public service of our satellites? Is their world not still our world, the world we built, the world that relies on this good and singular Earth like a child still relies on its mother even after learning to walk?*

She shuddered at the memory.

"Sisters?"

They both turned. A middle-aged woman in a habit stood a few feet away at the edge of a bed of roses. Mother Lucia examined her garb and tried to remember which order wore that sort of style. It had been a long time since she had been among enough different orders to have to match the cut of cloth to the particular saint. The Ursulines? No. Sisters of the Presentation of the Blessed Virgin Mary? Yes, that might be it. Though there was always the possibility that her outfit was simply what had been available at the time she needed a new one and did not even conform to the technical specifications of her order.

The woman nodded slightly at them. "I am Sister Marietta of the Order of St. Ofra. We saw your ship's docking code. I've come to offer you our hospitality."

Mother Lucia stepped closer, and now could see that

the woman was older than she had first thought. Not as old as the last Reverend Mother, but in her sixties perhaps. Though one aged differently in full-time gravity and she sometimes found it difficult to read the ages of those who had spent most of their lives on soil. Her face betrayed nothing else.

"You're very gracious," she said. News traveled slowly sometimes out here, but not slowly enough for the Sisters of St. Ofra to be ignorant of their group's severed relationship with the Church. Mother Lucia had still not had the stomach to learn whether or not they had been officially excommunicated or merely stricken from the rolls of support, but either way, all the religious orders would have gotten an updated list of which convents and bands were of the Church and could be trusted, and which could not. Was this merely kindness to travelers of a similar bent, offered freely and graciously? Was it an offer of support more materially? Or was it a trap—the ears and hands of a religious house bent to the purposes of Central Governance?

"It's as we have always done. It's been a long time since any of us were off-world. I am sure you come bearing stories." Sister Marietta put no particular tone on anything she said.

If this was an offer of aid, they needed it. If it was something else—well, Mother Lucia looked ahead and saw no appealing options. If this were a snare being tightened slowly about them, it was at least a good idea to see the rope.

"We would be delighted," she said, and Sister Faustina made the slightest bit of a face, but said nothing. "Let us call down the rest of our sisters. As you have been a long time on the ground, we have been a long time in space, and it would be lovely to share a meal with women of similar philosophy."

If Sister Marietta noticed her careful description of their relationship to each other, she made no comment on it.

~

The Sisters of St. Ofra resided in a small house on the edge of the campus, built in the four-walls-and-slanted-roof style popular in western Europe on Old Earth before humans had taken to the stars in any great numbers, more modern than the rest of the university was built to evoke but quaintly historical nonetheless. There had been some discussion about whether the two orders should share services before dinner, but the idea had fallen by the wayside—for the best, Sister Ewostatewos thought. They were less likely to offend each other with different interpretations if the only thing they shared was a meal and its blessing. How strange to think there had once been a time when humanity was so compact, and communication so instantaneous, that one could assume another Catholic had nearly the same readings and rites you did. As the spaces between them had grown vast, so had the variations in faith.

The lighting inside was all electric instead of chemlights. Sister Ewostatewos had heard that St. Ofra had advanced hydroelectric facilities, but she hadn't expected no chemlights at all. The strange white light made her eyes hurt and showed everything too starkly. Maybe she had been too long out of real sunlight. Or maybe this light just evoked a long-ago sterility that made her skin crawl. Eris settled in between her and Kristen like a second shadow, which was not helping things.

The Sisters of St. Ofra were only five women.

"I wasn't aware there *was* an order on St. Ofra still," Mother Lucia said, as they all sat down around a table that looked like it might have been built from some of the prefab material off the original ships. In an alcove in the corner, an icon of Mary looked down on them, hands spread, a sparkling rosary dangling from her right. "Are you involved in the running of the school?"

The mother superior of the Sisters of St. Ofra was called Lavinia, but it was Sister Marietta who did most of the talking. At first Mother Lavinia's silence made Sister Ewostatewos nervous—it was too much like the old Reverend Mother and her mysterious vow—but Mother Lavinia was younger, and it became clear quickly that she was merely reserved. And possibly, by the way the other four took the majority of the labor for her, possessed of a physical ailment that limited her energy, but that was not the sort of thing you inquired about with a stranger.

"We're not involved," Sister Marietta said. "Though we have our own small preparatory academy here. The original sisters of our group were brought along by the university's trustees mostly as, ah—"

"Window dressing," provided another sister, a young woman who then bit her tongue.

"Yes. A useful way to secure funding, in a time when most of the civil institutions on Earth had closed their pocketbooks. And the university has become overtly secular in the decades since. We leave them to their own affairs, and they to ours. The financial maintenance of our order is a stipulation in their charter, otherwise I am sure we would have been asked to leave long ago."

Mother Lavinia sighed, and lifted her soup spoon with some effort. She dipped it into the broth the sisters had laid out before all of them, and placed the single spoonful carefully into her mouth. "It is an unusual situation," she said. "But most of ours are unusual out here, aren't they?"

Sister Ewostatewos watched Mother Lucia stir her

own broth, clockwise and then counter, like there was some fortune to be found in the speckles of fat and skin at the bottom of the bowl.

"Please," Mother Lucia said. She lifted her spoon, but only an inch or two above the broth, coming nowhere close to her lips. "Let us speak plainly to each other. I've found I've had my fill of double meanings and coded phrases this past year. I am sure you weren't so eager to ask us here simply out of a feeling of sisterhood. You know what we have done; you know, surely, the request we made of the university's trustees."

Sister Marietta stared down into her own bowl, and dabbed her dry mouth delicately with the edge of the linen napkin. Mother Lavinia continued to stir her soup. The other Sisters of St. Ofra said nothing. One lifted her own bowl and drank it down in a sharp swallow. Sister Ewostatewos looked to Sister Faustina who, for once, seemed as unsure as the rest of them and steadfastly refused to touch her own food.

The large figure of Mary in the brightest corner of the room seemed to loom over them. The orangeish electric lights turned all the painted reds to bright, bleeding scarlet. From this angle she could see that the icon was Mary in her Our Lady of Sorrows incarnation, with seven thin golden spears piercing the wooden breast. The red *was* blood, soaking down her front, pooling beneath the sandals and brown-painted feet. Was St. Ofra a Servite order? She couldn't remember, though that didn't sound correct. Though things like orders and origination tended to get muddled this far out. It was not like the first system, where you were likely to have reliable communication with a mother house and a perpetually updated set of rules for your order. For one: enclosed orders were rare here, in this system where free water and free air were rarer than gold on Earth, and so many orders who were cloistered back in the relative safety of the first system found it necessary to work in the world in this system in order to provide for their worldly needs. Was a discalced Carmelite still a true member of her order, if she lived in a ship that could not be enclosed, because it needed supplies from orbital stations and maintenance from workers outside the order? Sister Ewostatewos was not a scholar, so she did not particularly care about the answer to that question. But Rome did, she was sure.

Something about the icon made her uncomfortable, as did the silence, which was now stretching beyond what could be called a contemplative pause.

"We too wish to maintain a certain independence," Sister Marietta said, finally. "Over the years we have found a way of life and worship that works for us. Were Rome to take a firmer hand..." She looked at Mother Lavinia who seemed to have nothing but a dreamy displacement in her eyes. Again that small disquiet settled in Sister Ewostatewos's stomach, but how many people found their own order, with their matching black habits and strict routine, equally disquieting? Faith was such a private thing, no matter how much structure the Church believed it could impose. "Well. We share your concerns. Let us leave it there for now."

"We appreciate your sympathy," Sister Faustina said coldly. Mother Lucia touched her hand, and Sister Faustina's other fist tightened around her spoon. Another mystery, that—their new allegiance. Many bonds had been broken and reforged in the crucible of their past year, but every time Sister Ewostatewos saw those two bent in a private confidence she was surprised.

"We *do* appreciate it," Mother Lucia said, and for once Sister Ewostatewos saw a struggling ember of that fire that had once stirred in her friend so often. "But we would appreciate more your action."

"You've already benefited from it," said Sister Marietta, and this time the Sisters of St. Ofra shared a small, secret look somewhere in between guilt and pride. "We have been monitoring the ships in orbit independently of the university. A Central Governance ship docked two hours ago. It claims to be carrying two scientists to participate in the genetics conference, but the energy expenditures and reported supplies would suggest a far larger force on board. I have personally taken the liberty of rearranging your own ship's logs in our records and the university's to obscure its exact position, but that measure won't stand up to much scrutiny."

"Thank you," Mother Lucia said, but Sister Ewostatewos heard the sudden panic strain her voice. This *had* been a trap. Or become one.

"We are also worried about our students," Sister Marietta said. She pulled something from her pocket, a folded piece of paper, and slid it across the table. "Few of them may come to us for guidance anymore, but they are still our charges."

Mother Lucia took the paper and unfolded it. Nothing changed on her face but the air seemed to twist, a cold draft in the stuffy room. She handed it over to Sister Faustina, who held it out for the rest of them to see. A poster, cheaply printed, a moon cast in bleeding red.

WHAT WAS DONE WILL BE DONE AGAIN, it read. WITHOUT THREE SYSTEMS UNITED.

"This is the least direct of the ones we've found," Sister Marietta said. "Some of the others speak of a martyr, a holy Reverend Mother who died to give us a chance against ringeye and a warning against Central Governance."

Sister Faustina closed her eyes, shook her head.

"I did not know your last abbess," Sister Lavinia said,

"but I assume that you are not trying to canonize her already. There's a meeting of the *faithful* tomorrow. Using the conference as cover to gather, I imagine. Their self-proclaimed Moses is coming down from the mountain."

"We'll go," Sister Faustina said. The poster fluttered in her hands.

"No," Mother Lucia said. "I'll go. No need for more than one of us."

"But—"

"We can discuss it more later." Mother Lucia didn't need to look over at the Sisters of St. Ofra for them all to know she meant *when we're alone.* "Sisters—the university trustees turned down our proposal to release our archives from Phoyongsa III with their support and sanctuary. Your influence may be limited, I know, but perhaps you could intercede . . ."

Mother Lavinia lifted her trembling hand again, and shook her head. The broth sloshed over the lip of the spoon and when she finally raised it high enough to meet her mouth it couldn't have been enough to do more than wet her lips. "You are the infamous Sisters of St. Rita. We would like our life to go on as it is, but you are the ones who struck this match. There are too many ways this could go for me to risk my sisters. Surely you understand that."

~

She had promised discussion, but in the end Mother Lucia decided not to allow any. This was her right as the abbess, she told herself, even as she saw Sister Faustina smolder and Sister Varvara doubt her. She went alone to the meeting of the faithful.

The university hall from the pamphlet cleaved to the same style as all the others on the campus—the same style she imagined was the standard of second-tier universities on Earth whether it be England or Beijing. Old enough to be old, but not enough to be ancient, accomplished enough to be impressive but not enough to merit an architecture all its own. Red brick, modern curving windows, a little ways out of the center of the university and rented to anyone who wanted it. Through the smoked glass doors, she saw people moving around inside, many people.

Mother Lucia stepped into the packed room and looked for a way through the crowd—there were dozens of people here, more people pressed into each other than she had seen in months now, and she was far too short and slight to bully her way through to the front. But the crowd parted for her in her habit like that biblical sea. One woman wearing a strange vacsuit, all silver and blue like the rarest elements—was that from the fourth system, where the customs had grown even stranger still?—reached out and touched the edge of her sleeve with a child's thoughtless fascination. They thought she was a part of this, clearly. Perhaps she was. On the wall someone had pinned up a long banner with the image of a moon over a planet—the moon radiant and haloed, a promised land, the planet merely the backdrop for its glory. Something in a plastic jar sat beside it on a ledge. Mother Lucia could not face the front of the room yet, so she turned instead to the jar. It smelled even from a foot away lightly alcoholic, like the old-fashioned anatomical specimens she'd seen in a museum as a medical student in a life long ago. It was a section of flesh, one side gray but intact, the other torn with the cells burst. Frost damage. She knew the structure of it, had spent years now learning the way muscles like that worked. Ship's flesh.

She was suddenly dizzy. The jar had an adhesive label but she thought it best not to read it.

The murmuring crowd had grown quiet. The back of her neck prickled. She straightened up again and turned around and the people (postulants? pilgrims?) again parted for her. At the front of the room sat a woman draped in a long pale-gray tunic; hair bound up in another length of cloth, black this time; a real-wood cane with a shining brass head leaning against her thigh; boots poking out from under the layers that looked like surplus from some struggling colony's underfunded militia.

"I saved a piece of it," the woman said, this newfound,

star-grown prophet. "Do you miss it?"

Mother Lucia thought about the *Our Lady of Impossible Constellations,* the warmth of its embrace, the way its breath had held and caressed her during those hours she had spent inside of its deepest parts caring for its growing young. She touched the jar, but it was only cool and dry, nothing like the beast itself. She did not know what she'd expected to feel instead. Dead flesh inside a jar could only feel one way.

No—she knew what she had expected. This was a relic; she had expected to touch it and feel holiness reaching back, despite everything she knew. Some scripts were just bound up deep in humans, she supposed. If a thing looks holy, is wrapped in the presentation of godliness, you expect to find a god inside.

"I do miss it," she said.

"There's more than that. You could take one back with you. A gift."

"Thank you." She let go of the jar and felt nothing, still. "But I'm not sure that the sisters would find that—comforting."

Terret smiled. It was only with that smile on that Mother Lucia saw anything of the woman she had known. Before this moment she had hoped she had been mistaken. Terret's pilgrims looked from one woman to the other uncomfortably—they could feel the frisson in the air but did not know the story of it. Mother Lucia wondered how much she was a character in Terret's new parable. If she told this crowd her name, would they see her as another kind of icon for their devotion?

Terret stood up. Her pilgrims spread around her, keeping a respectful distance. She took the two steps down from the chair leaning on her cane, but her stride was surer than it had been when the sisters had parted ways with her family on that nowhere station months ago. Still, she was different in a way that could not be explained just by the lingering effects of ringeye. She seemed older, but not old. She wore a religious habit and smock, but the style of dress didn't fit exactly any order or sect Mother Lucia could name. It felt constructed. Like the story of a saint that had never existed, written by combining the common tropes of hagiography with the correct structure, a very good story without any history beneath it. Yes, that is what Terret felt like now. A well-crafted myth.

"Would you like to talk?" Terret asked. Her voice seemed to carry, reverberating back on them off of every wall. One man behind her tilted his head, examining her. Mother Lucia thought she recognized him—the deputy chief from the orbital station where they had spent the six months after Phoyongsa III letting the neophyte ship grow to a habitable size and attempting to brush away any trail that Central Governance could follow to find them.

"It's why I came." Mother Lucia looked past Terret's shoulder to the crowd arrayed behind her. Terret smiled again, but not as nicely this time.

"Come then," Terret said. "Our ship will be more private."

~

Terret's ship was less a ship than a shuttle. Mother Lucia doubted it had a range long enough to reach the next habitable planet. She looked around the small front chamber, but saw no evidence of a man or child. And for a prophet, the room was unusually clean of any iconography. A hatch led to the rest of the ship, but Terret did not offer to show her beyond it. Two gray chairs—mass-produced military surplus like Terret's boots—a cabinet, and a touchscreen were all the furnishings the room would allow. Terret gestured at the chairs with her free hand and Mother Lucia sat. Terret opened the cabinet and took from it a bottle and two shatterproof glasses. She poured and Mother Lucia drank what she was offered. A kind of wine, she supposed, and it went down acidic and rough. Nothing at all like the honeyed wine they had shared that first night on that ill-fated moon. The same ritual seen again through a cracked mirror.

"Where are your sisters?" Terret asked.

Mother Lucia sipped the wine again. It went down no easier the second time. "Where is your family?"

"Safe elsewhere."

"We had thought you were intending to keep yourself safe as well." The shatterproof glass was too light. She wanted something hefty to grip, something that would be satisfying to throw. She made herself set the glass on the arm of the chair.

Terret swirled the liquid in her glass. She hadn't had any of it at all. "That was the whole idea of the moon, you know. Start our own colony, carve a safe corner out of the universe. Hard work, good people, build a life with our own sweat and blood. In retrospect—you never are truly alone in the universe, are you?" She too set down her glass, and leaned forward in her chair, elbows on her knees. She had such bright eyes. It was impossible to look anywhere but deep into them. "I am sure you find this all quite gauche."

"Captain, I am not even sure what *this all* is."

"I'm hardly a captain anymore." Terret laughed, a sound that set Mother Lucia's teeth on edge. "Now I'm a prophet, apparently. It's all so much easier than I thought, truly. Shockingly easy. I understand why Central Governance has decided to tie itself to the Church now. Such an available weapon, and so simple to wield. Come now, Mother, don't look at me like that. I've done more to unite this system against Central Governance with nothing more than my own sad story and some well-chosen iconography than any politician has done in the forty years since the war." She gripped her cup, lifted it, finally drank. "What more godly cause can there be than that?"

"You have made a saint of a war criminal!" Mother Lucia smacked the arm of the chair and her glass went flying, splashing the pale, burning wine across the sterilized metal floor. Terret didn't flinch, didn't say anything at all. "You have taken a woman who killed thousands, who lied to all of us, who spent her life hiding behind a wimple from any consequences for the chaos and blood she brought, and you have made her into—into someone to be *prayed* to! A holy intercessor! Down there at that university I saw a student with her face on a poster like—like—"

"Like she was deserving of it?" Terret asked. The spilled wine spread to the toe of her boot. "Do you not believe in redemption?"

"Of course. God's redemption. We are all unfortunately only fallible flesh."

"Your trust was betrayed. My friends were murdered. Which of us has the right to this story?" Terret reached down, picked up the cup, and righted it. It still sat on the metal floor in the pale wine, a strange break in the pattern of the light that cut the watery white of the inorganic bulbs into jagged rainbows. She shifted in her chair, crossed her good leg over the bad, tilted her head to Mother Lucia like this was just an easy conversation, like they were two old friends with nothing between them but a lackluster vintage. It was then that Mother Lucia saw the strange box. She had mistaken it before for hardware. Just a chromed, slim case, the length of a tablet stylus and a few inches wide. But it was not a piece of hardware; it was too perfectly displayed in the center of the room's only cabinet. Something about it hit an old part of her brain, but she could not name the quiet unease that unfurled within her.

Terret followed her gaze, and settled back in her seat. "You'll not want to hear about that yet. Maybe it is better for us both if you leave me to my plans, and you and the sisters can disappear into the black as you've been trying to do."

"We haven't been—" Mother Lucia started, but of course they had, or at least she had. Trying to pretend they could simply fade into the mendicant wandering they'd had before, the simplicity of medicine and babies delivered, of blessings bestowed for crops and quick healing and nothing wider than that. "Tell me."

"It's a reliquary."

Impossible. The outer systems had so few saints of their own, and fewer relics still. St. Ofra might have some in their archives and museums, but such places did not sell them to upstart prophets. The case, she realized, was just the right size for a finger. But whose—

"You do intend to make a saint of her." Her throat seized, it came out a whisper. The part of her brain that had spent years reading medical textbooks and dissecting the bodies of larger and larger beings said that it would be very convenient to divide a body that had been frozen in a sunless bit of space. The cell structures would be well-preserved but most of the liquid gone. She closed her eyes and saw the Reverend Mother, disintegrated, the parts of her sent across the known universe as a call to revolution. Saw her in life, welcoming a younger Lucia aboard with a kind hand on her shoulder. Saw her before she took the habit, watching a solar system burn at her gentle urging. She could not make the three different women into one. The wine turned sour in the back of her mouth. She wanted to say, *You have no right,* but how could she? The woman she had thought belonged to them—who had taken her in, who had talked to her for hours of God and His works, who had seen her in tears and in joy—that woman was only a story she had told herself. She had not known the Reverend Mother at all, not really. "Why don't you see how wrong that is?"

"You predecessor is dead, she won't care. And if God cares I won't know until I follow her, unless He sees fit to grant me a vision like one of your chronicles. So until then I must do what I think is best."

The enormity of it was overwhelming. Mother Lucia tried to imagine this future, the future where alongside Hilda and Theresa and the other saints sat an icon of the Reverend Mother. Where someone might kneel on the floor of a prefab chapel in a moon beyond imagination, in a fifth and yet-undiscovered system even, and look up at the cross and think of the half-remembered, much-distorted story of a long-ago saint who had been a murderer and then a nun and then a righteous martyr to the cause.

"Would you like some more wine?" Terret asked. "I do not drink so much myself anymore. But some moments do call for a drink."

"No, thank you." Again Mother Lucia searched for the woman she had known, who'd captained her ship across three systems, who had spent years arranging with careful certainty a world of her very own. Well, the arranging was the same, she supposed. The elegant planning and the follow-through. Merely bent to a different end now. "Terret. I understand—you and Joseph worked so hard to build a life for your son, and Central Governance destroyed it because all you were worth to them was the same as a petri dish. I know how much you must want to protect your son. How you must want to avenge the future he would have had."

One of Terret's eyebrows moved up ever so slightly. She lifted her cup and sipped again at the wine, though the level in the cup did not seem to change no matter how much she put it to her lips. Only the air moving through the ventilation system made any sound at all. Terret rubbed her thumb around the lip of the cup. "Do you know what?" she said, and that cold, sculpted dignity she'd worn like a mantle this whole time vanished. "Not one second of this is for my son."

Terret set the cup down on the cabinet with a definitive *clunk*. "I love my son. But he has never imagined a better future. He will have the very best life he can build for himself and yes, I hope this makes it better than it otherwise might be. But it is my world that was destroyed." She gripped the arm of the chair so hard her knuckles went white. "*My* life's work. My years of toil and planning. I was supposed to have a world that I built, with the people I loved, and it would have been perfect. And in some things, my dear Mother, we have only one shot in life no matter how much we want to believe otherwise. My window is closed. That future is dead. And yes, I would like vengeance. Not for my baby. For me. For who

I should have been."

She twisted her hands together and Mother Lucia realized with a bone-deep shock, a shock she should not have felt at all, that the newborn prophet was trembling in her chair. When Terret spoke again her voice was low and as jagged as the ice crystals that clung to the bare rock of the asteroid where Mother Lucia had spent her childhood. "I understand you're grieving. Quite deeply, I'm sure. But do not come here and tell me that the loss of a ship-beast and a woman who never told you a true thing in your whole time with her is the same as watching the door close on the only life you had ever wanted, the life you had molded yourself for until it was the only shape you fit." She stood abruptly and Mother Lucia leaned back, even though the idea that Terret would lay a hand on her was inconceivable. The woman radiated rage. No—righteous fury. Just like a saint. This could be a scene in a hagiography—Mother Lucia saw it in her mind's eye as clear as anything, the righteous woman confronting the disbeliever wearing the mark of religious authority. It knocked her back in her seat. It made it hard to breathe. Suddenly she was tilted and spilt out of her body, watching this whole scene as history, as another twisted story rewritten to prove a moral that real life would never be clean enough to fit inside. She felt cold sweat slick her palms.

"This is a weapon," Terret said. "Our lives, what happened to us. And I will wield it, as it's the only one I have. Aren't you angry, Mother? For the life you and your sisters should have had, for your certainty? Stand with me or don't. But I know you understand me."

Mother Lucia rose shaking from the chair, but nothing came to her. Behind Terret's eyes lay only steel and stone and those stolen futures. She turned and hit the hatch button to let herself out—there was nothing else here for either of them.

~

They had all, without any kind of discussion or conscious agreement, gathered in the hydroponics chamber. It was the first of the main rooms of the ship after one entered through the cargo bay, which meant that Mother Lucia would pass by them. Sister Ewostatewos tended to a bed of carrots while they waited for their abbess to return. If the others saw her shaking hands, they would think it only the same nervousness the rest of them held. One of the tubes that brought nutrients from the ship's digestive tract into the beds had clogged with sediment and she cleaned it with a fingernail. She felt Eris's attention on her back, hot and insistent, and refused to turn around to look.

The floor beneath them hardened almost imperceptibly, the ship tensing its muscles as the main hatch opened and shut. Then the soft sucking noise of the inner hatches opening one by one. They all, together, looked to the hatch they'd left open, and Mother Lucia crossed past it a moment later.

Sister Faustina was on her first. "Well, Mother?"

Their abbess jumped. She had to have seen them—the grow lights in the hydroponics bay should have cast them all starkly. But on her face was genuine surprise, mixed with something darker and dirtier. Eris saw it too—and Sister Ewostatewos saw that look on her sister's face like she smelled blood in the water.

"Surely no one is telling the true story," Sister Varvara said. She'd always been one to make up her mind and never let it change. "This is all silly rumors. Some lonely people playacting religion put together with scraps they've heard."

"Or it's Central Governance itself," Sister Faustina said. "Attempting to draw us out, or control the narrative. But it cannot be sincere."

Mother Lucia came into the hydroponics bay, but stopped right over the hatch. She held something in her hand, a leaflet, crumpled and murky now.

"Why shouldn't it be sincere?" Sister Ewostatewos asked, and heard the bitterness in her own voice. "We tried our best to keep this quiet, and could not, and we should have known that it was too big to keep hold of."

Across the room, Eris smiled. She had followed Sister Ewostatewos all day like a malignant shadow. If this was her way of begging forgiveness, it was not very effective. And clearly she knew how she had Sister Ewostatewos trapped—the person in her wanted to leave Eris here when they departed, but the religious sister in her had a duty to help those in need, and the scared child that was still there somewhere deep down would rather pull her fingernails out with her teeth than explain to her sisters all of the terrible things they had done. Especially after how Mother Lucia had reacted to Kristen. She could feel the life she had so carefully built for herself crumbling beneath her, back into wreckage and dust and blood.

Mother Lucia went to the place on the ship's wall where two expanses of moss met in a darker line, opened the seam to the waste recycler, and dropped the paper inside for the ship to turn into mucus and hemolymph.

"It's Terret," she said. "She has turned her colony's death into a gospel, and the Reverend Mother into a saint, and there are many who believe she is going to lead them into a great just universe where they no longer have to fear Central Governance's boot."

Sister Ewostatewos turned away to hide what crossed her face—in her stomach it felt like a mix of anger and disgust and cold, sick confusion. The silver fish they kept in the beds for fertilizer and to keep the algae down—none bigger than her pinky nail—darted away from her shadow. One lingered in a forest of white roots. When Sister Ewostatewos dipped a finger in to shoo it, she realized it was dead.

Sister Faustina huffed the way she did when she had found one of the universe's small horrors. "Why? She's as much—more—at risk than we are. Her son too."

"Her son is apparently safe somewhere on an un-mapped planet." Mother Lucia finally came into the room, and sat heavily on the bench in front of their seed storage. "And she, well, Terret is angry. She was meant to lead a world. I suppose it's not incredibly surprising she has decided that, since that was taken from her, she will lead a revolution instead."

"And she convinced all these people," Sister Varvara said. "Dragging them all into the danger she only nar-rowly escaped? And after she knew what the Reverend Mother did. As if she's the picture of holy redemption, when she chose to die rather than answer to us." Her voice dripped disdain.

"She has very compelling evidence," Mother Lucia said. "People are angry, too. Forty years since the war and still everyone waits with bated breath for the Central Governance to decide it wants to yoke us all again, and now to learn that the worst plague in historical memory is a weapon pointed at us? They're beyond angry. How many of you visited the museum at the Jesuit house in the Hermes belt?"

Sister Ewostatewos never had, but Sister Varvara and Faustina murmured their confirmation.

"Did you see the relic of St. Anthony of Padua?"

Despite never having seen it, Sister Ewostatewos could conjure it instantly. The mummified tongue and jaw smiling grotesquely inside a rock crystal sphere, balancing between a gold stand and halo. It was the most famous Christian relic outside of the first system, not that the outer systems had many of their own. It had disappeared before the war and was long thought lost, before it reappeared in a struggling habitat-bubble on what was then the remotest edge of the second system just in time to heal the sick and force the molding seedstock to sprout despite themselves. She didn't understand the implication and then, horrifyingly, she did.

"She didn't," Sister Varvara said. "To disrespect the dead like that, to sanctify—"

"Three fingers sheathed in silver alloy and cut glass. Though she doesn't yet claim they are performing miracles. And she has some ... pieces ... of the *Our Lady of Impossible Constellations*."

Bile rose in Sister Ewostatewos's throat. The idea of

the ship floating lonely and cold alone in the dark had haunted her dreams for months. As much as she had argued against the idea of it having a rational soul, the idea of its final, eternal rest being disturbed turned her stomach. A creature that had served them so dutifully and so well dissected to be pressed into service once more. The others went silent too, as silent as she imagined that lonely graveyard of Phoyongsa III was now.

"What are we going to do about this?" Sister Varvara asked.

"What can we do about it?" Sister Faustina replied. "She owns it as much as we do."

"And she will paint a target on us as much as herself!"

Sister Ewostatewos could see it. Central Governance would come again, the dull armor and ever-fanciful weaponry that had haunted her nightmares for years after she and Eris had escaped. At best, they would all die, and at worst, the rest of the four systems of scattered humanity would be dragged back into the great maw of endless war. There'd be plenty of martyrs then, enough for a whole generation of cults. Another generation of revolutionaries like flies attempting to hunt a lion, another generation of their children taken for the training camps. It never ended, did it? They hadn't escaped; they'd only found the eye of the storm.

"You tried to talk her out of it, surely," Sister Varvara

said, as if this was a matter of simple misinterpretation.

"She may not think she hears the voice of God," Mother Lucia said, "but I do think she feels herself one of His crusaders."

"Releasing our archives may protect us." A soft sound, like rubber—Sister Faustina pacing back and forth across the taut-muscle floor. "And her in turn. Rally popular support, so we are not just alone to be picked off without notice."

"And that *will* start a war."

"You all talk like war isn't already here." Sister Ewostatewos watched the dead fish sink to the bottom of the bed, where its compatriots would soon strip the flesh from its bones. "What do you think the ringeye was, except a volley? What do you think their training programs are, scooping up children by the handful? The fact that we have been able to pretend there wasn't a war doesn't mean it hadn't already come to us, quiet and in disguise. Release the archives—at least we would finally have a common cause."

She turned back to the others and saw the surprise on her sisters' faces. She so rarely spoke like this, she knew. But she felt emptied of everything that even resembled hope. Perhaps it had died with the *Our Lady* and now sat mummified in a canister in Terret's looking-glass chapel. Behind her sisters, Eris smiled at this acknowledgment that she'd been right.

~

The *Cheng I Sao* came through the thin asteroid belt that divided the settled fourth system from the frontier, and there, right as had been promised by every rumor and whisper Gemma and Vauca had collected as they'd crossed this young system, was the oily glimmer of the dwarf star's ultraviolet light scattering across the thick skin of a dozen ships.

"They're *here*," Jared breathed, even though he'd objected to this wild detour.

On instinct, Gemma looked at Vauca's face first, and saw that brilliant smile break across her face like sunrise. She sent a hail into the herd, but even from here on this junk-level viewscreen it was obvious these weren't crewed ships. They moved amongst each other, twisting and scraping each other in ways that would make any people inside sick. Gemma leaned closer to the screen like that might improve the resolution. "They're not rogue."

That shook Vauca out of her blissful reverie. "What?"

"Where are the comms arrays, the sensors?" All of the metal pieces that shipwrights bridled their charges with as they grew, which should be shining obvious silver and copper against that green-gray skin.

Vauca leaned in too, so close that her breath was on Gemma's cheek and her heart leapt for the touch of it. Three of the ships broke with the pack and swanned among each other, frills ruffling in what Gemma recognized as contentment. "They're not," she agreed. "Wild. Wild ships, how?"

Gemma studied the image. It shouldn't be possible. Larval ships had to be reared in low gravity, grown on a lattice that delivered essential nutrients directly into their systems and prevented their fragile internal structures from collapsing, then spoon-fed the vacuum until they grew a tolerance for it. Some kind of experiment? The fourth system would be the place for it, and there were certainly enough weird groups out here, including one that was pursuing a cyborg future and another that added silver to their water deliberately so all their skin was tinged blue. But a shipyard was expensive infrastructure.

These ships had small bulbous growths within their skin furrows, now that she was looking closely. Vauca peered at them too. "Organic technology? Maybe they're ... I don't know, some kind of fluid cushioning for the comms systems and that's why we can't see it?"

"It's the same color as the neonates," Gemma said. "Don't you think?" Stone gray and slick, absent the symbiotic chloroplasts that the adults absorbed as they matured.

The intercom crackled and Yevet said, "There's a few more down in the planet's stratosphere. You see them?" Vauca changed the zoom and focus on the screen and yes, there were two ships hovering in the thin atmosphere of the nearest roiling planet while a few others fluttered some kilometers overhead.

One of the ships low in the atmosphere shuddered and its body shimmered as brightly green as the sun through stained glass. It seemed, to Gemma's eye, like it was in pain or stressed at least. Then she saw it, small gray shapes still defenseless emerging from between the callused plates that protected the ship's soft underbelly. They flopped this way and that in the thin air before fitting themselves into the furrows in the mother ship's skin. Gemma found that she was gripping the rosary in her pocket so hard that the little hands of the crucifix bit into her palm.

"Look at that." Vauca practically pressed her nose to the screen. "What do you think that is? Some kind of mucilaginous secretion that seals them in? Or maybe like a reptile's extra eyelid?" Gemma found herself watching Vauca instead of watching the ships doing that extraordinary thing no human had ever seen done outside of their control. Her eyes blazed with awe, the true meaning of awe, something great and terrible and far, far bigger than either of them could ever comprehend in this single moment. She was beautiful. Heat spread through Gemma's chest, taking everything she might have been able to say.

"Something weird is happening," said Yevet.

"Yes," Vauca said, "we see."

"Not—" Their ship shuddered suddenly. Deadships did not shudder. "I don't think they like us." Vauca zoomed back out and yes, the rest of the herd had turned toward them, rustling their frills frantically. They moved toward the *Cheng I Sao,* much faster than Gemma had ever seen a liveship move of its own volition. One came straight on, but more broke pack like they were coming to surround the ship.

"They're protecting the birthing ones?" Vauca asked, as if that was not against everything they knew about the limits of liveships' intelligence and social communication.

The intercom crackled again. "The captain thinks we ought to—"

The ship leapt forward in space and Gemma jerked back. "Go!"

Jared hit the engines and the front of the pack recoiled from the sudden heat. Vauca ran to the engine room, which always had issues with hard starts, and Gemma went to the lab, because she needed to see all of her genetic analysis of the ships again, to understand how this was possible.

By the time she came up for air, it was the nightcycle. Dinner had come and gone, and she had missed it in a haze of DNA and shipyard behavioral reports. Someone would have left a plate for her, curried lentils and rice tonight if she remembered correctly, but any hunger she might have had was too quiet for her to care. She crept down the hall where her crewmates slept and knocked softly on Vauca's door. No answer, but the handle turned when she tried it.

Vauca was sitting up in her bunk, tablet in her lap. She set it aside when she saw Gemma standing in the doorway. She moved over and pulled back the covers, and Gemma crawled in next to her and laid her head on Vauca's shoulder like they had been doing this for the whole last year, like they hadn't been sleeping in different cabins, like Gemma had remembered all along how to touch another person. Vauca's hand cupped the back of Gemma's head, a very gentle question.

"It isn't your fault that I've—had a hard time being here," Gemma said, and the words echoed around the metal room. In a liveship, your words disappeared into soft walls. Here, they stuck around with you. "I wanted—I *want*—to be here. But I spent so long thinking that my life would be—a pair of hands to do God's work, I suppose, I don't know how to do this. And my sisters are struggling, and I cannot help them because I left them. I left the thing I said was my calling. And yes, I chose this, and studying the liveships is something I could do nowhere else and *you're* here . . ."

"Gemma . . ."

"That isn't my name either, you know. Or not the one I was born with. St. Gemma was a mystic. She thought God spoke to her. I thought it romantic." She licked her lips. There was that dryness in her throat again, but she carried on. "I'm not sure I'm worthy of her name any-more, but this is the name I've held for so long. My given name belonged to a different person, a child."

She thought she felt Vauca's heartbeat speed up in the hollow of her collarbone. She was a biologist, she knew the chemical reactions that caused this, but still it felt like some awful power to have this effect on another person. This was what scared her most, perhaps. To be bound to someone not by purpose or similar devotion or sworn sisterhood, but only a love that could not be bounded by rules or regulations and could be broken at any time.

"We both should have known this would be a hard adjustment. This is—a very different life," Vauca said. "I want to help you find who you are now."

"I'm not sure you can."

"I'd like to try, at least, if you'd let me."

Gemma closed her eyes, so the world was only the

touch and smell and sound of her. "Yes. I'd like that very much."

~

On the last morning of the conference, Mother Lucia, Sister Faustina, and Sister Varvara went down to the surface to try negotiating with Terret one last time. Sister Ewostatewos stayed behind. She had no wish to see the outcome of another person put through the crucible. And more than that, she was sure now that none of them could stop what was coming. Terret was building a quiet army to ride against the force of Central Governance. Neither one could stray from the course now.

She tried to spend the morning in the hydroponics bay again, with the feeds from the ship's cameras playing out scenes from the surface while she worked. The students milling through the university's central quadrangle looked like the fist-sized drones mining operations used to scout new veins, roaming in a pattern that seemed aimless but that hid a single-minded purpose. Sister Ewostatewos imagined some of them holding rocks or long bars of tungsten from the manufacturing department. Ready for a fight, ready for someone to flip their activation switch and aim them at the right target. Young enough to not remember the war themselves, old enough to suffer under the traumas of their parents, old enough to carry forward those old fears and vengeances. She had work to do, but all day she had been trapped in waiting, like God Himself was holding His breath.

Several of the ships in orbit—the Terran ones, she could tell by the way they gleamed with all-new parts—pulled back from the orbital docking station, and all at once that sensation of awaiting broke.

"Mother," she tried the comm.

"Something's happening down here." Mother Lucia's voice barely broke the background hiss—what was going on with their receiver? "Can this wait?"

"The Central Governance ships—they're moving. I think you should all come back." She saw their trajectory—headed to land right next to the crowd of students. Surely they would not fire on hundreds of children. Surely not. No matter what revolutionary fanaticism was being whipped up amongst them.

"After we find Terret. Don't worry—I see the ships—they're landing far from us for now. We'll be quick—" The link cut off in the pleasant *beep* that meant Mother Lucia had ended the call. *Don't worry,* she said, and here she herself was too worried for goodbyes.

Sister Ewostatewos watched the Central Governance soldiers emerge from their ship like fire ants from a hill on the auxiliary screen in the hydroponics bay. St. Ofra's defensive net arced over the university, flashing blue light, keeping the other two ECG ships out but trapping her away from her sisters. She had to get to the control bay—either get away from the ships out here or go down to help. The hatch sucked in behind her; she turned around and there was Eris, sweating.

"Always us in the end, eh?" Eris said.

"I have to get to navigation." She tried to slide past but Eris wouldn't let her.

Eris's warm hand gripped Sister Ewostatewos's. "We shall leave, the two of us. Somewhere far beyond their reach. One of the planets in the fourth system that's never even heard of Earth, where strange creatures run free and the water and the sky are the same color blue." Sister Ewostatewos didn't have to see her face to see her smile, because she knew the face that Eris made when she talked like this. The strained grin with a wild mouth and all her teeth. Fine enough when they were girls making up fantasies. Worse when they were on their own and Eris's impulses got them into the shit.

"I've built something here," Sister Ewostatewos said. All she could think about was what was happening on the surface, if the soldiers already had found Mother Lucia and Sister Faustina and Sister Varvara. She tried again to push Eris away.

Eris gave her wimple a little tug that yanked Sister

Ewostatewos's hair underneath it. "So many rules. Doing the same thing day after day, routines down to the hour, helping everyone but yourself. I have made for us a different life, another chance."

Something in her phrasing stopped Sister Ewostatewos cold. "What have you done?"

"In the fourth system, no one would ever find you if you didn't want them to—"

"What have you done!"

Eris licked her lips. "I lied to you," she said. "I told you I was on the run, but they had already found me. My blood matched yours in the Church database. They were already planning on hunting your lot down, after that cursed moon. I am only keeping you safe."

"You turned us in," Sister Ewostatewos said. "Gave us the right information, the right pushes, to bring us here where they were waiting."

"They would have found you anyway." Eris's hand squeezed her wrist tight. "But I made a deal. They will let us go, as long as we never come back."

"I know you don't understand." She could try to explain but it would be wasted breath. As much as Eris couldn't comprehend her faith, she had one of her own that she held just as tight. A prayer that they could run far enough to escape all Earthly trouble, and that in such a life they might find a pure joy and freedom that Sister

Ewostatewos had never been able to make herself believe in. She knew zealotry, had seen enough of it to know that there was no reasoning a person out of it. She could write a whole gospel about the small satisfaction of doing good work with her own hands and Eris would read it cover to cover and still not comprehend. She peeled herself away from her sister, tugged her hand back to herself. "I wish I could be free of you."

Eris's breathing stayed steady, hot. Sister Ewostatewos imagined she could feel her heart beating inside this hollow room, but she could not, of course. It was her own pulse echoing in her ears. Eris's would never race like this. Eris's heart only raced in the heat of the moment, like a hunting dog set on prey. Sister Ewostatewos had seen hunting dogs on a colony where they'd been asked to attend a delivery once, a weird fungal swamp terraformed by a funny little cult that liked their sea a soupy orange and their ground spongy underfoot. The dogs were lean and six-limbed, with a predator's set gaze. The colonists there set them on the natural fauna, a kind of small hare that wasn't adapting well to the new ecosystem. In those dogs, in their single-mindedness and their barely leashed bloody desires, she had thought, *There is my sister.*

"How could you be?" Eris asked. Not *Don't you love me?* Or *After all we've been through?* They were beyond love, into a strange trajectory of orbital decay and joined bodies. "Your fate is mine. We began together."

"No," Sister Ewostatewos whispered. She saw that last day, three years after they had escaped the training camp, when she had watched Eris sell her services to a second-system cartel for money they didn't need. Because to Eris, the end would always justify the means. "I'm a different person now. Your sister died when I put on this veil. It was—a whole other life."

Eris shook her head fiercely. "No. There is a revolution coming—I've been part of it!—you have to come with me."

"Aren't you lonely?" Sister Ewostatewos asked.

Eris faltered. For a moment nothing burned in her. "Why do you think I want you to come with me? We're supposed to be together."

"I was still lonely when it was the two of us." Sister Ewostatewos prised her hand free. "Have you ever seen the gardens on Wisteria Moon? The horticulture sculptures, where all the trees have grown together into lions or chairs or fairy-tale castles?"

"You want to talk about gardens?"

"The trees are spliced together. Back a long time ago on Earth, they'd be pruned and bent over years to make the shape. But the trees on Wisteria Moon are bits of this and that, the different species' growth rates forcing them into a pattern in months. They're beautiful, of course, but eventually the splices give. Either the different trees split and grow wild again, or they die." Sister Ewostatewos watched Eris carefully out of the corner of her eye, her shadowed outline bending itself into different angles to pretend she hadn't heard or didn't understand. In this dim room, it was just like childhood again, those many nights when Sister Ewostatewos had put herself to sleep counting Eris's breaths alongside the whispery puffs from the ventilation system and the distant noise of footsteps in corridors beyond their bunks.

"No one else knows what we've done," Eris said. "Who would you talk to?"

"I don't want to talk about it anymore." And she didn't, she discovered. For years those times had lingered in the back of her mind, a secret she always feared she was on the verge of telling, equal parts dangerous and shameful. But in the years since she'd turned over cell by cell into a new shape, and this new person felt nothing for it. It was a long time ago, in the orbit of a different sun, under the record of a different name. She had killed one man, who did not deserve it, and God would judge her for that. But she could no longer judge herself.

"I thought I would always have you," Eris said.

"I know." Sister Ewostatewos expected Eris's nails to dig into the tendons in her wrist and hold her so tight that she wouldn't be able to tell which pulse was whose.

But the space in between their bodies grew cold instead. Eris's tongue clicked against the inside of her teeth like she might try another argument.

"You won't be safe from what's coming," she said, finally.

"No," Sister Ewostatewos agreed. Eris's hands slipped away. "No one will. None of us can control it."

Eris laughed, a strange sound. "Well, I'm going to try to, if you won't come with me. You always did dream too small, sister."

"I would not mind to see it." And she would not, as much as she knew that Eris's visions were cloaked in frisson blasts and spilled blood, depressurizations and implosions. Someone had to wage a war with fire. Let each give as they were able. She could not find it in her to condemn it. If Eris tore a path through the four systems in pursuit of justice, then she would follow mending what was left behind, and there was still a kind of symmetry in that. Not the suicidal decaying orbits of binary stars, but still two bodies that felt the pull of each other's gravity.

She went for the door again, and Eris let her past. She needed to find some way to get her sisters off the surface.

When she tried the hatch, it wouldn't open. "Eris," she said, and smacked the button again. "Please."

But all that showed on Eris's face was confusion, and that chilled Sister Ewostatewos's blood. She tried her comms to call down to the others, and got only an empty feed.

"You're not doing this?"

"No." Eris tried her own equipment, and from her building frustration, Sister Ewostatewos knew that she too had been locked out. She tried the room's auxiliary controls again—tried to change something small, the air recycling rate, which should be possible from here. The ship did not respond. She beat the hatch button with her fist. Nothing.

They had been hijacked. It was the only explanation. Sister Ewostatewos took a deep breath. Comms down, trapped, ship control locked. She had to get word down to the others.

There was one thing to try. She found a penknife that she usually used for scoring seeds, located a particular spot on the ship's inner wall, and cut through the mucous membrane. Mother Lucia would have her head for this, cutting into the ship with an unsterilized blade. The thought of it was calming, actually. It presumed a future where they were all alive and well enough to argue over mundane things like a ship infection. If she was right—and she might not be, she had neither Mother Lucia's biological expertise nor Sister Faustina's knowledge of the communications systems—they were close to one of the embedded transponders that allowed the ship to connect with the relay networks.

"What are you doing?" Eris still sat in the corner, hunched over. That same caged animal look as their last years in the military camps.

There, beneath a sinew sheath—a tangle of cabling and a node. "I am going to try to use this system to call down to my sisters. We shouldn't need permission from the central array to send a short-range message if we can access the hardware directly." She tried to summon that long-forgotten security training. Some ships, she thought, did have fail-safes for this sort of thing. But that was an expensive upgrade she doubted Mother Lucia had agreed to. On a liveship, one generally tried to reduce the complexity of the mechanics as much as possible, given that any extensive maintenance required surgery rather than just opening a few wall panels on a deadship. She pulled the node out into the air and tried to ignore the slick swelling, the bright green fluid, and the shift in the ship's heartbeat. She would apologize to it later. Feed it a treat of extra sugars.

"I didn't realize nuns were so—hands on."

"What is it you think we do, Eris? Rock babies all day and sing songs? This isn't Earth, we can't live in a beautiful garden full of free oxygen and sing hymns behind a screen." She'd have to say a prayer for that as well, speaking ill of her sister-communities. But right now she felt nothing for them but frustration. It seemed the easy way, making prayer your only work. No matter how many afflicted you asked intercession for.

She wiped the node clean with the edge of her sleeve. There should be a way in. But of course, knowing a thing was possible was not the same as knowing how to do it.

"Let me." There was Eris beside her. "That's old enough, I could take it apart."

Or destroy it. Take whatever Central Governance had promised her and flee before their snare closed again. She—they—had done it before. And yet, uncertainty was better than certain defeat. She handed the node over to Eris, who turned it around and around.

"You're really never coming with me, are you?" Eris said. The transmitter glistened in her hand, vulnerable.

"No. I'm not."

She tried to read Eris's face, but she had always been so good at hiding what was beneath. Where Sister Ewostatewos had cried and screamed in their first months in the schools, Eris had turned to silence, waiting and waiting until she tried to stab a private with a knife she'd stolen from the edge of a lunch tray on its way to the recyclers. Once, Sister Ewostatewos had been able to read these stillnesses, but there were many years and many leagues between them now, and Eris's face hid as much as the surface of a dark lake.

Eris finally pried open the node, and fiddled around inside until she had found a particular piece of circuitry. "This is the short-range transmitter. You should be able to connect, but I'd do text over audio. The change in data leaving the ship will probably be visible to whoever has control of the comms." She placed the open box carefully in Sister Ewostatewos's hands. Something formed on her face—the beginning of a telling emotion—another plea perhaps—but she shook her head and said nothing.

"Thank you."

Eris turned her face away.

"No—Eris, really, *thank you.*" For more than this, but whatever she meant, Sister Ewostatewos couldn't hold it in words. For freeing her, for how they had lived through it.

The placid surface of Eris's face broke and there for an instant were sorrow and hope and grief. "Of course."

~

"How many years has it been since those were active?" Above Mother Lucia, the strange blue electricity of the university's perimeter defense system crackled.

Sister Marietta peered out from underneath the portico and that war-shock look flickered across her face. "Thirty-four years, more or less. It was up all through the war and then a few years after, til people stopped jumping in their skins at every unknown ship." She put her hand on the door and shook her head at the both of them. "I'm sorry."

"You have a duty to your students," Sister Faustina said.

"Many duties to keep and we're all running out of hands to keep them with." Sister Marietta nodded to them once and then the abbey door closed behind them.

"We can't stay down here." Sister Faustina rubbed her hands together. Even her nervous tics said *get to work*. Mother Lucia sometimes wondered how she had honed her whole self toward utility. "If we go to the ship . . . they're much faster. I would like to believe the university board would turn out their security force for us, but they've not exactly run to our defense so far."

Mother Lucia felt for the rosary at her side. Was that what they were down to after all this? Prayer? The university would do what it had to do to protect its students. Central Governance would do what it had to before the Phoyongsa III story and Terret's own tale spun further than they could control, a window that was fast closing. Whichever force won, neither was on the side of the sisters.

Her comm buzzed—a short burst for a ship message.

"It's Sister Ewostatewos," she said, and Sister Faustina

settled. She opened her mouth to say hello but it wasn't live. She had to listen twice before the meaning could make its way through the blood boiling in her ears. "The ship's not an option."

"We didn't think it was."

"No, it's been—she and Eris are locked in the lab, locked out of communications—someone's hijacked it." The ship—the one permanent thing they had, the last thing left of their lives from before, before *all this*—someone had taken it from them. Before they could even get to know it. She imagined it helpless there, waiting for them to come back, crewless and as confused as an animal could be without its purpose.

"Mother." Sister Faustina's hand was on her arm, and her heart was skipping in her chest.

She pulled herself free, pointed up at the sky where she imagined it was waiting for them. "If Eris is with Sister Ewostatewos, there is *one person* who remains to have done this."

The look on Sister Faustina's face said she had come to the same conclusion. "That's an issue we can't do anything about planetside."

Mother Lucia closed her eyes. That hot brilliant thing that had been simmering inside her this whole raging year threatened to break the bonds she'd put on it. "I told you—I told you we could only rely on each other."

Sister Faustina said nothing. The students streamed around them, some running for the cover of dorms or classrooms, others with the crazed excitement of young people who didn't know any better yet thinking they were headed to righteous battle. Metal shutters came down over the windows, the doors bolted shut.

"Go find Sister Varvara and Terret," she said. Sister Faustina hesitated. She knew she looked a mess, she could feel the sweat on her forehead and the hot flush of anger creeping up her neck. "Go. I am going to try to reason with our postulant."

"Sister Varvara and Terret will be together—are you sure you want to be left alone with her?"

"It is my ship now," Mother Lucia replied. "My responsibility is to it and to all of you. I am telling you as your Mother Superior—go make sure the others are safe." Sister Faustina and Sister Varvara and Terret all together, she would keep the three of them as well as she could. And not let Sister Faustina listen to her try to beg for the lives of the others up above.

When she called up to the ship, the main line still worked. So Kristen had not frozen out all communications, only the outgoing ones she didn't authorize. Mother Lucia tried to take that as a good sign. A true zealot would have left only the channel between her and her commander open. And apparently she did not know that Mother Lucia had permission to open the intercom without her having to answer. When she did, the hiss of static filled up her stomach as heavily as dread. She strained to hear something—anything—on the open channel. The ship's breathing, even though she knew that the mics were calibrated to cut out that background noise. Sister Ewostatewos, perhaps, even though it would likely be her pleading.

~

The station came into view on the *Cheng I Sao*'s screen like another sun, painted bright yellow and gold by someone with a very particular aesthetic. Werrin had called this station's crew *odd ducks* and declined to elaborate further. Vauca had let on that they had some very unusual beliefs that came from someone's reading of Egyptian alchemical texts. Old texts, the kind that had been ancient even before Earth had started being called Old Earth. The station was crowded for this system—five deadships all lined up in a row, hanging from its xanthic skin like leeches. Gemma had missed the bustle out here. Perhaps they could stay a day or two. Surely a station that venerated the old Egyptians of the pyramids and the one Sun would have a puppet theater or live music.

"I have a feeling this guy's going to try to renegotiate,"

Vauca said. She and Yevet were checking over the inventories one last time. This had been a difficult commission, no use in showing up with the wrong thing. "All of these specific requirements plus the haggling over our rush rates? Don't you go soft and give him a deal, Werrin."

One of the ships docked at the station lifted off, but hovered close. It was bullet-sleek, a newer design than often made it all the way out here to the edge of humanity. Gemma had more often seen ships cobbled together with parts of derelicts from countries and colonies that no longer existed—the Holy Lunar Empire, that stillborn experiment neither holy nor an empire; the Assembled Free States of the Gate, the brief guardians of the jumppoint to the second system; America, whose end was lost with their archives.

Werrin relayed their identification key again and received the final approval to dock.

The comms panel chirped. Gemma reached for the button to ignore the message, but read its tag—it was marked as having been sent at the highest urgency. Someone had paid handsomely to send it via private networks rather than the public relays, bypassing all of the usual delays and circumnavigations, accelerated in the jump between systems, so it would reach them directly and nearly immediately.

"Look at that." Vauca whistled, and pointed at the hovering vessel. "You never see ships like that out here. Beautiful."

The message was only text. Smaller file size, quicker to convey. *You do not know me but I am abbess of the Ursuline community on St. Ofra. Your ship's identity and position has been released to Central Governance and they are no longer content to wait. For confirmation—your friend told me that your first gift to her was a bookmark.*

"Turn around," Gemma said. "Lucia sent us a message—those aren't—"

The bookmark had barely been a gift. She had lost Lucia's her first week on board—absentmindedly fed it to the ship along with all the other table sweepings—and given her a new one. But it was the kind of insignificant thing no one but them would ever know.

Across the station, extra shielding slid down over hatches and joins, the things you covered when you were expecting weapons fire outside your front door. That ship—too new, too dangerous—lingered.

The *Cheng I Sao* had more defenses than the Order of St. Rita's convent-ship, it was true, but that was like saying a fruit fly was possessed of greater intelligence than a potato. Jared reached for the controls for their only torpedo system but Werrin stopped him. "They don't know we see them yet."

The short-range comms chimed. "*Cheng I Sao,* your identification has been verified. You are approved to dock."

"Thank you," Werrin said, while he slowly adjusted their heading, switching each necessary system over individually so that a consolidated energy surge wouldn't show up on the other ships' instruments. "Could you retransmit the docking procedures? We are having some issues with our receiver."

The person on the other end made an anxious noise that might have sounded like annoyance had they not known what was coming. So Central Governance had gone to threats rather than bribes. Gemma scratched at her collar, suddenly sticking to the back of her damp neck. Vauca was ashen-faced, frozen, gripping the console. Yevet choked on something in their throat.

"I'm going to—" Werrin said, right before the hard acceleration knocked all their feet out from under them.

Gemma rolled onto her stomach. The stars streaked across the viewing screen, the resolution unable to keep up with their current speed. Werrin pulled himself up to sitting. They should be in their beds or chairs for this speed. Two hundred years earlier the acceleration would have killed them. Even with the modern dampeners Gemma's teeth rattled with the pressure building inside her head. "Where did you send us to?"

"Our last coordinates. Easiest thing to reach for."

Something crackled and the ship shuddered.

"Are they shooting at us?" Vauca asked. "With hard projectiles? At speed? Are they mad? They blow us up and fly right into their own debris field."

"Only a warning shot," Werrin said. "Listen—they'll overtake us sooner or later. They don't need to risk blowing us up here."

The comm crackled.

"Ship *Cheng I Sao*," said a woman's voice. They'd hijacked the comms. Of course they had. This ship might be advanced for this system, but it was built out of ECG parts from a generation ago. "Stop and prepare to be boarded."

Yevet pulled themself up. The dampeners were starting to match the acceleration. "By whose authority?"

"Stop and be boarded." The woman must have been standing close to the mic. The audio hissed and popped.

They were not intending to appeal to any authority but the right of their overwhelming force.

Gemma got to her feet. On the nav screen, the *Cheng I Sao* was a brilliant red line against a black vacuum. Behind them, a yellow line tracked the trajectory of their pursuer.

"How long do we have?" Jared asked.

Werrin stared at the calculations, trajectory versus fuel

reserves versus speed. "We're going to hit the gas giant in . . . three hours? Fuel will be almost gone then."

He was only off by twenty minutes, though not in their favor. The ship rattled constantly now, like a fevered body. The low tremors shook Gemma's bones inside her skin. They were running out of fuel—the ship was running too hot, too inefficiently, burning dregs and fumes. Ahead of them, the wild herd's barren moon loomed. They were out of road too, and with no safe harbors to sail to. The wild ships swam around the moon like a small cloud system, gray and green like storms, and it was not, Gemma thought, the worst view to see when you died.

"I don't know where else to go," Werrin said. "We could land and try to hide out, I suppose."

"They just have to wait for us to run out of air," Jared said.

Their distress signal beeped sadly again. Gemma imagined it echoing out, past the lifeless moon and the unknowing wild ships, to the stations and traders and colonies that had all, surely, been paid or threatened to not send help when one small ship begged for it. Not that there was any time left for them to reach the *Cheng I Sao* now. She touched the wall behind her, closed her eyes, tried to pretend that she was back on a ship that would hold her in its warmth and whose heartbeat she could lose herself in.

Jared ran the same numbers over and over again on his tablet, hoping it would come to a different result. Vauca stood braced against the nav console, watching their pursuers close in with the uncaring ease of predators who knew their prey was limping bleeding across the prairie and it was only a matter of time. Gemma went to stand next to her, so their shoulders were touching, and covered Vauca's pale-knuckled hand with her own.

"Can't believe they came all the way out here," Vauca said, and shook her head in a kind of awful wonder. "We really are a danger to them. Us, this little ship."

Gemma suddenly saw Vauca, an hour from now or maybe two, floating dead in space, the star at her back turning the droplets of blood off her body into steam, the debris of the *Cheng I Sao* around her like a halo around a saint in the old pictures. She closed her eyes against the image, but her mouth still tasted like acid. When she opened her eyes, she saw that Vauca didn't have starcharts open on the console as she'd thought, but one of their old letters. Her eyes fell on the beginning of a line and filled in the rest, just as fresh in her mind as when she had written it: *To give up a duty like mine is no small thing, it has shaped my entire life, my entire self; it took the iron of me and forged it into steel.*

"I'm sorry," Gemma said. Vauca intertwined her fingers with hers. "If it weren't for me—" She stopped, for the guilt of it was too much for her voice to carry. "Do you regret the letters?"

Her heart thudded in the long second it took Vauca to answer. "No. Never. I do regret the future we might have had. I was just thinking of all the people we might have become together, had we had a chance to shape each other."

The ship groaned and the recycling air turned tinny like the steam at cheap heat-tray cafeterias on the big stations.

Vauca hesitated, squeezing her hand. "Do you regret giving up the life you had for me? I know it has not been . . . comfortable for you."

"No," Gemma said. "If I have to die today, I'd not do it anywhere else."

On the main screen, the Central Governance ships continued their implacable approach, like watching the bullet fired from the gun aimed at you, and Gemma was surprised to find she meant it as much as she had ever meant anything in her life. As much as she had meant her vows, even.

~

The first thing Mother Lucia heard over the open line was Kristen's breathing, frantic and hard.

"We trusted you," she said into the open line, and then winced. Not the best start. A student stopped short in front of her, wearing a shirt emblazoned with a hand-drawn bloody moon—she recognized him from Terret's gathering. She glared at him until he too ran for the safety of one of the dormitories. At least not all of them were eager to throw themselves in front of an army.

"Kristen," she said. "This is not the only choice you have. Sister Ewostatewos and her sister are up there with you. If you do what I imagine you are planning, they both die. By your hand, no one else's."

Another long silence and then, as if from far away: "This is the mission I was given."

"You told me your father died in Central Governance's service, and now you'll serve the same master? Or was that a lie as well?"

She heard the chirps and beeps from the ship's system. They had buried the archives from Phoyongsa III deep, but Kristen would find them eventually. Especially if she had the comms and engineering experience she claimed.

"Most of it was true," Kristen said. The ship's system made an angry noise and she hissed through her teeth. "But I was . . . younger. And for all my parents' talk of communes and family, when our money ran out, I was old enough to be sent out on my own. Too young for anything, though. Except the military. You must understand,

Mother. This life of yours—it isn't so different from mine. A place to belong, a mission. I'm sorry. I wish it were different. I wish . . ." She trailed off into an unnamable want.

So that's what it was. Not money, not security, not a fervent belief in Central Governance. They had given the girl a family. Mother Lucia could not think of how to offer something worth more than that.

She closed her eyes and tried to find some golden words, some divine inspiration that would tell her how to reach across the gulf of this one trembling line. She had been told she had a gift for kindness once upon a time, but that was different from this. She did not write homilies, was no bishop directing a whole flock. She wandered and offered what little she could.

"You saw what we did, Kristen," she said. "I know Sister Varvara showed you. You have done nothing yet that cannot be undone. Please. We can think of another choice together."

As the frantic, screaming students streamed around her, she prayed again for someone else to take hold of her tongue and give her what she needed. But she was only one woman, alone on a path on a world that was not her own, waiting to see if the entirety of her life was about to fall burning from the sky.

~

Sister Faustina found Sister Varvara, as she had hoped, banging on Mr. Dominguez's door. Campus security was ringing the administration building, but apparently wearing a habit still got you through some doors. Sister Varvara gave her a look that said she was close to doing some things that would break their vows if the trustee did not let them in.

The door opened.

Dominguez was out of his Spanish costume, wearing a school T-shirt that made him look like one of his students. His beautiful office now seemed a charade, all the books, all the fancy imported wood only playing at power.

"You people," he said, and jabbed a finger at them both. "You people brought this here."

"This was always coming," Sister Varvara said. "In one form or another. You think when Central Governance decided to return, they would let the university stand independent?"

There was something else mixed into the anger on his face. Guilt, maybe. His phone lay thrown aside on his desk, like he'd just tossed it away after a conversation gone awry. "They didn't agree to your terms now, did they?"

Sister Varvara knew better than to show surprise. Sister Faustina pointed at the phone. "You have a duty to your students, you have the contact information for every ship in your airspace. I am guessing the first thing you did was ask if they would leave you alone if you handed us over. But they want more than just us."

"I do have a duty to my students," Dominguez said, and Sister Faustina was actually surprised to see tears in his eyes. "These are children, most of them. They don't remember what the war was like. Most of their *parents* don't remember what the war was like. They don't know how hard it was for us to survive, in the hopes that when it was over, we would still be here for the system. Whether you believe me or not, I see the same future you see, where we can be more than scattered colonies and stations. But I won't be the one to bring another dark age down on my students."

"Many of your students are currently arming themselves with pipes and chemistry sets because they don't plan on allowing their university to be occupied by Old Earth," Sister Varvara said, and it was Sister Faustina's turn to jump. She glanced out the window and yes—there were students, milling around in groups, not running for safety but wearing the grim determined looks of people who believed they served a righteous cause. Terret *was* a prophet. She had seen a war and here it was. She'd made it with her own two hands.

"You have enough armaments to repel them this time," Sister Faustina said. "They will go through your students. This afternoon will become another bloody rumor haunting the relays. Please. Buy us all some more time." She pushed his phone toward him. One call. All they needed.

Mr. Dominguez put his head in his hands. She had thought him younger than her but now she could see that that was only artifice. He was, in fact, old enough to remember. He took the phone from her.

~

Sister Ewostatewos stopped at the edge of the comms room. Kristen sat in Sister Faustina's chair, too short for it, so the curving slope of the gelatinous growth hit right at the edge of her skull. She was still wearing the postulant's clothing they'd assembled for her, which made the whole scene take on a profane glow. She hadn't turned on the chemlights, so the room was lit only with the orange-blue-green softness from the biolumenescent algaes grown in thin membrane tubes around the top of every chamber, and it cast deep shadows under every bone on Kristen's face so that Sister Ewostatewos felt as if she was seeing the skull under the skin.

Eris had disappeared somewhere else in the ship. No time to think about that now.

"Kristen," she said. Kristen's head didn't move. On one screen there was a man's face. By the stripes on his uniform's shoulder, he was a colonel. Kristen's colonel. Sister Ewostatewos didn't recognize the patch that said where in the four systems he was stationed. Not from Earth, at least. On another screen, Kristen had the file from Phoyongsa III up. She would have to kill them, to clean all traces, but Sister Ewostatewos was sure that this was already the plan. Kristen could take a vacsuit out the hatch and be pulled in by the ECG ship in minutes.

"I can't force you to make the right choice." Mother Lucia's voice crackled over the comm. "I can only hope and pray for you."

"Have you finished wiping the archives?" The man on the screen narrowed his eyes. The sort of look that Sister Ewostatewos and her sister had been trained on, the kind that offered the pride and reward they craved if they behaved and promised punishment if they did not.

"I'm trying," Kristen said, though her hands weren't touching the controls. "They have more security than a nunnery should."

The colonel snorted. "Should've expected as much, two thousand years of keeping their secrets." He said something indistinguishable to someone off-screen.

"Should've ended all this nonsense after the war, when we had the chance . . . let the outer systems keep the gods and leave us to actually get things done."

Kristen said nothing. Her hands hovered over the controls.

"Work faster," the colonel said. "Do you need me to send you more people? We're having to pull people off the planet—the university has forgotten who feeds it. Without their archives, the sisters have nothing to back up their wild fairy tales."

The hairs on the back of Sister Ewostatewos's neck prickled. She looked over her shoulder. Eris stood behind her, holding the heavy kitchen rolling pin. She shook her head, but Eris was fixated on Kristen. A fine sheen of sweat dusted Kristen's forehead and she wiped it with the edge of her sleeve. And then she caught Eris's eye in the reflection of the main screen.

"The other operative you have on board," she said. The colonel grimaced. Sister Ewostatewos assumed that meant Eris had not been easy to control. "Someone's encrypted their files. It looks like one of our systems—has she turned?"

"Fuck," the colonel said. "If she has—"

Eris stepped out from behind Sister Ewostatewos, over the threshold, and into view of the camera. Sister Ewostatewos tried to catch her sister's arm, but Eris shrugged her off. Kristen turned, too slow and still, Sister Ewostatewos thought, to defend herself. But then she didn't know Eris.

"Eris," Sister Ewostatewos said. She wasn't sure what to say next. *Don't spill blood on this young ship of ours,* maybe, like the ship was a child.

Eris brought the bludgeon down. Sister Ewostatewos turned away, toward the pulsing green wall. She'd seen so much death, but it never got easier to stomach more. The audio from the colonel's ship went to static and then cut dead.

"Good choice," Eris said. "I would not have given you a second chance to duck."

Sister Ewostatewos turned back. Kristen's head was pressed against the back of the seat, eyes closed, but there was no blood. She was crying, Sister Ewostatewos saw. The fronds cushioning the neck of the comms seat reached up to lap the salt water from her eyelashes. Salt and water, necessary for life—the ship would draw these bits of her into itself and turn them to heat and light.

Eris pressed her thumb to the control screen. The audio channel briefly reopened. "Do you want the body back, Colonel?" Around the ship, across the vid screen, the university's energy net finally encircled them. The colonel did not bother to reply.

~

The Central Governance ship approached, lazily advancing on the *Cheng I Sao*. There was nowhere to run, no one even within distance to help. They could take their time, make sure that the explosion was contained. No sense spreading debris across a perfectly good stretch of space, now that they'd gotten far from any witnesses. No one out here to see the ships and log their identification codes. This last stand would not become another tale of martyrs for the revolution to be spread in whispers across failing satellite networks and relays.

The liveships outside circled around their herdmates, showing the brighter green of inner frills here and there. They'd been stirred up too. Even these great beasts, never touched by humans in their lives, could sense that danger had come to their doorstep. One of the larger ones gathered the trembling adolescent ships into itself.

"I wish we'd been able to understand them," Vauca said. Her hand stuck damp to Gemma's. In the failing lights, Yevet was bent over their station, head down over praying hands. "That might be the only thing I'll really regret. All they might have told us . . . it could have been the greatest discovery of our generation. A fairy tale for children, living right here on a moon no one will ever bother to colonize."

A ship full of Central Governance conscripts wouldn't understand what they were looking at. Old Earth had long abandoned liveships anyway. Too slow, too idiosyncratic, prone to strange resistance. All of the things they didn't understand would remain mysteries, until this system filled more perhaps, and someone got curious again. One of the larvae gestating in the furrows of the mature ships glowed briefly—what was that? A growth spurt? Communication?—and Gemma's heart squeezed tight at the sudden longing that seized her down to her bones.

"Take us into the herd," she said.

"What?" Werrin was glued to the vidscreen, watching their approaching death. "You'd rather die by their hand than Old Earth's?"

"Please." The idea that had half formed inside the most wishful part of her couldn't be spoken aloud lest it turn to nothing in the air.

Jared shrugged—what was a different death?—and emptied their last reserves into the engines. Straight ahead, nothing difficult to chart there. They leapt into the middle of the herd. Gray-green bodies filled the vidscreen; one of the ships hit them sideways and the whole metal skeleton of the *Cheng I Sao* shuddered and groaned.

The vidscreen was completely covered now—they couldn't see the ECG ship now even if they wanted to.

"What the fuck was this supposed to accomplish!" Yevet shouted.

The ship lurched again. Gemma reached for Vauca again, but now she was across the room.

"The larvae are waking up," she said. "Way more active, all sorts of weird hormones and neurotransmitters coming out here. These bigger ships..." She looked at Gemma and broke into a grin. "Did you guess this?"

"Guess *what*?" Werrin said.

"They don't know what the ship itself is," Vauca said. "They probably think we're like ... an inconvenient rock. But they know what the larvae in our pods are. They think we're a bunch of lost hatchlings."

The vidscreen might be useless, but the scanners weren't bothered by a few hundred meters of gelatinous musculature. Gemma watched the dot of the Central Governance ship hovering uncertainly just beyond the herd.

"I'm turning off the power," Yevet said. "Hide our energy output."

The screen went dark under Gemma's hands. They were right, but claustrophobia suddenly held her tight. The lights went out, and the hum of the air recycling systems went silent. The only noise in the world was the soft, terrified breathing of her crew. She stepped carefully toward where she thought Vauca was, and found her arms outstretched and waiting. Vauca was shivering, though the room was still pleasantly warm in the after-glow of life support. Gemma held her tight, and tried to memorize the steel and musk smell of her, in case this was her last conscious thought in this life. She tried to think of a prayer for a time such as this—she'd read so many martyrs' stories after all, terrible deaths in habitat-bubbles leaking air or frozen wastelands with other dead around them—but could not think of anything. She prayed to have another day, and that was all.

Something exploded right outside. A torpedo. Gemma knew the sound, the almighty crack that always sounded like it should have an echo but couldn't out here where sound didn't travel. The ship rocked, but not as much as it should have. She didn't need the vidscreen to know they were being held tight within a pod of live-ships right now, held close like the prodigal son returned. She imagined them dying out there for them, creatures that had no concept of torpedoes or anti-craft deterrent systems even as the officer inside the ship took aim at them. The ship rocked again and again and again. Strange noises echoed down through the hull. A kind of crying out, she thought. She and Vauca were pressed so close—nails digging into skin, breath to breath—that she did not know where one of them ended and the other began. In the dark, waiting to see if they would die, there was nothing between them.

She would never know how long it went on. No more than minutes, though each stretched into a lifetime. When the final stillness came, she thought she might actually have crossed from the living to the dead without recognizing it. But no, the others slowly began to move, clothing rustling, ragged breathing evening out, someone's sniffles.

Yevet found their control panel and began to bring their systems back online one by one.

"Do you think—" Jared began.

"If they're still out there, we're done for anyway. Might as well see what's happened."

When the cameras came on, the vidscreen showed them covered in a film of light green fluid slowly evaporating in the unfiltered radiation of the faraway sun. Gemma didn't need to be told what that was. Shreds of shipflesh drifted in a cloud of viscera and animal terror all around them.

"Oh my God," Vauca said, and had to press a hand over her mouth. "How many of them do you think . . ."

"Look at that." Jared pointed out beyond the decimated liveships, and their bereaved herdmates turning distressed circles through the graveyard. Debris striped clean silver and scorched black spinning in the frictionless expanse. And then the bodies—an arm, a head, ice crystals collecting on an undefinable chunk of flesh caught in the shadow of one of the asteroids. Hemolymph and gasses from the dying liveships mixed with the evaporating last words of a dozen men in a cloud of droplets and ash. "They tore it apart. Can they—I did not know ships did that."

"They have the muscular capability, I suppose," Vauca said, though it sounded like it stuck in her throat. "I don't think there's much—call for it, when they're human-piloted."

Gemma had to close her eyes. She couldn't name why at first—they were safe, now, and so narrowly—but then the image of the *Our Lady of Impossible Constellations* shredding itself on the body of a warship above Phoyongsa III flashed through her mind. There'd been no burial for the *Our Lady* or the Reverend Mother, and there would be no burial for these nameless ships. She had vowed once to lead a life that healed instead of harmed, and now she had done the same thing as the woman whose fathomless past haunted her. She'd saved the people she loved; she had cost the grandest of creatures their lives. There were no good choices, only lesser evils, and she would not make another such choice for the world, but each gutted ship was one she'd have to atone for.

Vauca touched her hair, swept a wayward piece of it off her damp cheek. Gemma saw it in her eyes too, the awfulness of this, and the gratitude.

~

Far below, the sparkling habitat-bubbles that surrounded St. Ofra dimmed, and Sister Faustina had never been gladder to see an atmosphere disappear. She pressed her hands into the rim around the screen and the ship obligingly held them close. Yes. It was good to be back inside a heartbeat. Perhaps they would turn the gravity off tonight, after evening prayer. Then they would truly be home.

"May I?"

Sister Faustina turned. Mother Lucia leaned against the wall beside her without waiting for confirmation. The ship reached out to her as well, the symbiotic moss's fronds cushioning her shoulders and tickling her neck. She stroked the spot of wall next to her and the moss turned slightly pinkish beneath the green as hemolymph came to the surface. They were close to the center of the beast here, near its coddled organs. She tilted her head, it was Mother Lucia's ship as much as it was hers, and technically, they were supposed to have no privacy between each other. No matter how many silences and secrets had pockmarked these last couple of years.

"I've been thinking about where we should go now."

Sister Faustina chuckled. "I would prefer a good distance from another university. Too many politics, too much money in one place. There's a reason I never wanted to visit Old Earth."

"I've been considering the fourth system. Meet up with Gemma, perhaps. And there's not enough medical facilities even for people who can pay." Mother Lucia looked at her, though it wasn't in that tentative way where she quietly wanted Sister Faustina to tell her what to do. She was in charge now, fully. It was a good enough plan. The fourth system needed as much help as it could get.

"There's a war coming."

"Yes. As far as the fourth system maybe."

"People will need help here too."

A small smile crossed Mother Lucia's face, like a shadow on a blinding afternoon. "Wherever we go, we'll help people. It depends how close we want to be to the fire."

"We lit the spark, maybe we should be here for the flames."

"We didn't, though. This is older than us. I just hope it doesn't outlive us."

Sister Faustina looked back at the viewscreen, but they were far enough away now that without changing the parameters the university had vanished from their view. Somewhere down there, the students were building interplanetary coalition plans and the trustees were calling together governmental leaders from across the third system. Though there were plenty who were suspicious of how close the school was tied—or had been—to Earth money. They had come so close. After Phoyongsa III, after this, she didn't know if she'd ever sleep deeply again. "When you spoke to Kristen, did you feel it finally?"

Mother Lucia didn't have to ask what she meant. The silence stretched long. Mother Lucia twisted the gold ring around and around her finger. Wedded to God forever, but He was often a quiet, stubborn bridegroom. "No. I didn't. No golden light, no divine words on my tongue. If there was a hand guiding me, it was the gentlest touch." She cut off, but before Sister Faustina could say *I'm sorry*, she continued. "But it's all right. I used to think that faith was this great light in the darkness. A lighthouse to show me the way no matter how stormy the sea. But that's not it, is it? It's more like . . . a rope to lead you out of a dark cave. Sometimes you hang on tight. Sometimes you might drop it and have to scramble to find the lead again. Sometimes it feels like a line in the dark isn't enough. But it's always *there*."

Now it was Sister Faustina's turn to smile, though she felt it come and go as swiftly as Mother Lucia's. "I'm not sure I know what you mean."

"Even after all that."

"Even after." Sister Faustina squeezed a handful of the ship's moss and its heartbeat thudded through the palm of her hand. As long as it breathed, they did. "We are who we are, I think. Even after something like this comes and . . . changes our path."

In the next chamber, she heard the squish and hiss of the passage between the hall and the chapel opening and closing. Mother Lucia pushed herself off from the wall. It was time.

Everyone else was already in the chapel. Sister Varvara and Sister Ewostatewos in the front pew, Eris sulking in a dark corner half-hidden by the protuberance of one of the ship's main veins, Kristen in the very back row sitting as small as she could. Even Terret, shed of the long cloak and the rosary and the other accoutrements of her performance, standing near enough to the front of the chapel that the altar's shadow fell over her feet.

"You came," Sister Faustina said to her.

Terret inclined her head. "I've never been inside one of these ships, did you know that? And I wanted to see this. I was there for the old one's death and this one's birth."

Mother Lucia went to the altar and the tabernacle, just a small steel door they'd had to pay extra to have set into the wall between the ship's muscle fibers. On Earth, it was nearly Easter. On the desolate rock where Sister

Faustina had grown up they'd had no spring, and she always felt about this period like the world was holding its breath. She took her seat in the pew, crossed herself, and tried as she did every time to find that warm, warm light that was supposed to come, and just as every time before, she felt mostly an ache in her knees and the soft heat from the ship's metabolism, and just as every time before that was enough. They sang together, and prayed, and the ship breathed in their words. Mother Lucia passed the paten and she set a small square of bread on her tongue—the same bread they ate for toast now, not the unleavened wafers the Church had sent—and thought, not for the first time, what a miracle it was that she had this life instead of the one she had been born into. How long she had survived. No matter what came next, she'd survived far longer than this world had meant her to.

At the end of the service, they all sat in the hush for a long time. Sister Faustina listened to her sisters' breathing and their quiet, worried rustling.

"All right," Mother Lucia said. "It's time. The ship has gone long enough without a name."

Sister Varvara had been keeping the list, and she read it to them now: *Our Lady of Good Counsel, Our Lady of Prompt Succor, Our Lady of Mercy, Our Lady of Seven Sorrows* . . . in the list Sister Faustina heard the whole rise and fall of their last year, the hope and the grief.

"*Our Lady of Peace,*" Sister Ewostatewos suggested.

Mother Lucia shook her head. "Knowing what we know? That seems like a curse. It is traditional to choose a title of Mary, but we don't have to. *The House of the Rose*? For Rita?"

"Not many roses out this far," Sister Varvara said. "*The Undoer of Knots.* Something to aspire to."

Sister Faustina laughed. "I'm not sure anyone would say we've made a simpler world so far."

"How about *Refuge of Sinners*?"

Sister Faustina turned to look back at Terret, who shrugged. Behind her, Kristen and Eris, and over them, an icon of an anonymous Byzantine saint that an old man on a drought-stricken moon had pressed on them. And of course, they themselves, hardly saints, a collection of the sometimes-faithless and the sometimes-sharp and the sometimes-scared. "I like it."

Sister Varvara considered, and nodded, as did Sister Ewostatewos. "Something to aspire to as well."

They put it to a vote, the four of them, and every hand went up readily. Sister Faustina rolled the sound of it around on her tongue, *Refuge of Sinners*. Yes, there'd be refuge needed, soon enough. And before that, they needed to build the rest of themselves, the doctrine and rights and responsibilities they'd follow now that there was no one above to set it for them. But that was work for another day.

"Will you be staying for a meal?" Sister Faustina asked Terret, as they filed out of the chapel.

"I don't think so."

"You're welcome to it."

Terret shook her head. "There's work to be done. The war is already here, no matter how quiet it is, and we've got to face it together out here for once." She turned to Eris, still standing apart from them, so close to the wall that the moss thought the gravity was off and was reaching for the whole side of her body. "If you'd like a chance to undo what you've done, you are welcome to come with me. We can use your narrative skills. With a good story and a good propagandist, the whole system will hear of us."

Eris did not smile. Sister Faustina had noticed she rarely did, at least out of happiness. "I don't particularly believe in atonement."

"That's between you and whatever god you care to take."

Eris looked down the ship's long hall, and her gaze fell on Sister Ewostatewos. Such longing there, the way a child looked at the nice teacup they'd broken and now knew would never be whole again. "All right. I can't promise I'll stay for long. But you do have an effective strategy. Maybe the best I've seen to unify the system."

"You know I'm not much for the idea of divine judgment," Sister Faustina said. "But you *are* making a martyr out of a woman who never atoned for anything, and who died before she could ever answer for herself. I do find something . . . unnerving about that. You're burying the truth of her."

Terret tilted her head, and even without the long coat and the carefully selected gold and a congregation in front of her, Sister Faustina saw how she could stand in front of people and command their belief. "You yourselves are making a new sect here. And I don't think you can say you're doing it for any less worldly reasons than I am." She held out her hand to Eris, a welcome, and then led them toward the exit hatch like this was her own ship. Mother Lucia turned, and saw them leaving, but let them go with silence.

In the central chamber of the ship, where they did most of their living and doing, Sister Faustina folded the table down from the wall while Sister Ewostatewos and Mother Lucia brought out the food they had prepared earlier. This was not a feast, not exactly—religious orders did not tend to christen their ships with sabered sparkling wine and decadence the way some captains still did like their ancestors had with seafaring vessels. But it was an *occasion*. Fresh fruit, so difficult to keep here. Rice enlightened with garlic and dried herbs. A fish that Sister

Varvara had brought up from the university's wet market still alive in a cellulose tank, now steamed with more garlic.

They sat, and said grace, and ate with the relish of people who knew that there were harder times coming. Their plates were mostly empty when Mother Lucia poured more water into her cup and said, with a practiced carefulness, "Kristen has asked to join us."

Sister Varvara made a doubtful sound in the back of her throat. Sister Ewostatewos stayed absolutely silent and still. Sister Faustina looked at Kristen, whose hands were shaking as she gripped her table knife. Mother Lucia gave her a nod.

"I understand if you don't allow it," she said. "I've betrayed your kindness terribly. And done—unforgivable things, in service to an unforgivable cause."

The silence stretched out. Mother Lucia crossed her hands. She'd decided, clearly, that her leadership would not be iron-fisted.

"You're right," Sister Ewostatewos said. "You have served unforgivable causes."

"Are you voting no?" Mother Lucia asked.

"For now I'm noting the facts."

Sister Varvara considered the last bit of fish and rice on her plate, then sighed and pushed it away. "Tell us why you want this."

"I can't claim some ... divine call." Kristen's mouth worked without words and she rubbed at her jaw like it would shake something free. "I don't know if I possess a great well of faith. Not the way I've heard some of you speak of. But I want to do better. And it seems to me that this is a life where I can do that."

"We've always placed a higher value on good works than devotion," Sister Ewostatewos said.

Mother Lucia looked down the table. "Sister Faustina?"

Of course they would call on her, to judge a petitioner of dubious faith. Sister Faustina considered the pile of small silver bones on her plate, all that remained of the fish's contribution to their life. Deep down, she did believe that this was what would remain of them as well: bones and memories. Kristen was watching her, a nervous tremble in her eye. So young. It was hard to believe she herself had ever been that young, but she had, of course. Young, naive, desperate.

"This can be a hard life sometimes if you lack a faith to carry you through," she said. Especially now that they stood outside the protection of the Church. When she was young, she had joined for the promise of steady meals and quiet, and neither of those were promises anymore. She returned Mother Lucia's gaze. "Or if your faith wavers."

"I can't swear it won't. But I'd like to try."

"Let her try," Sister Varvara said. "This is one of the benefits of writing our own rules now. We can set a long novitiate. Give her—and us—time."

"Then we vote," Mother Lucia said.

Kristen dropped her eyes to her plate. Sister Varvara raised her hand, and then Sister Ewostatewos. Sister Faustina considered, and then raised hers as well. "If we're to live up to the name we've given our ship." And finally, Mother Lucia nodded.

~

In the fourth system, they said, anything was possible. Planets with orange skies and the strangest creatures you'd ever seen. Possibility itself, out here, far from Earth and its inheritance. Gemma had always found this a silly fantasy. Wherever there were people Earth's legacy followed, with all its joys and fears. But here, out in an asteroid belt that no one but unmanned drones had ever mapped, she understood how people could think that.

Four liveships twirled between the ice and glittering dust, smaller than the ones they'd seen closer to the center of the system, but still the same happy lichen-green. No larvae here, not yet, but two of the small herd worried at one asteroid, swishing aside the vapor cloud around it.

"What do you think they're doing?" she asked.

"Lots of minerals locked inside those asteroids that are hard to get out here." Vauca's head rested against her shoulder. They had set up a stream from the *Cheng I Sao*'s external cameras to Gemma's tablet to watch from Vauca's bed. There was a limit to how much they could fine-tune and direct the various sensors from here, of course. But it had been a long, long year, and the blankets were warm, and for a moment the only thing in the world was Vauca's foot against hers under the covers and the puzzle of wild liveships. She was learning how to enjoy these moments finally. This life was beginning to feel like it fit her. "Do you think they're cooperating? Problem-solving together to mine it?"

"That'd require a level of intelligence beyond what we think they're capable of. Well, beyond what we think shipyard-grown ones are capable of."

"When we write this up, there'll be plenty of opinions." Their last article on the mere existence of self-sustaining wild herds had caused a firestorm in the loose network of biologists, engineers, and shipwrights who studied liveships. The great beasts had been mysteries, but now they were mysteries within mysteries, the wild ones offering up a whole new puzzle. And here they were, their little ship, their little life, on the cusp of it. The joy of revelation that Gemma had thought she'd lost.

There was much to come, she knew. Another long darkness where the universe held its breath. And yet there was wonder still, even here, in a spray of rocks and ice in a sky that was anything but empty.

Acknowledgments

In the acknowledgments for the first book about the sisters of the Order of Saint Rita, I wrote that no book is possible alone. That is doubly true for *Sisters of the Forsaken Stars,* which was begun in one world and finished in another—from the early days of 2020 to sometime mid-2021. This past year and change has included both some of the greatest successes and greatest sadnesses of my life, and I could not have gotten through it without the people in my life.

It would be impossible to name everyone who was important to me during such an extraordinary time, but the sorely incomplete list includes: my friends, both those old enough to feel like family and those new enough to surprise me all the time; the queer SFF writers who have helped me find a community and also taught me so much; my work colleagues, both the mentors and those who just offered me a lot of slack in a weird time; the various experts who answered my questions about slugs or space or niche theology; the readers who sent me kind notes about *Sisters of the Vast Black,* which meant more than they could know; and of course, the creators behind the books, music, and art that I turned to through this year.

There are also a number of people on the publishing side whose hard work built this book from an idea to the copy in your hands, including many whose names and contributions I don't know. Those whose I do include my editor Christie Yant, who always has a great eye and notes that cut to the heart of the story; my agent, Hannah Bowman, who has provided much sage advice and encouragement; Emmanuel Shiu and Christine Foltzer, the artist and designer behind this beautiful cover; and Christina Orlando and Emily Goldman at Tordotcom Publishing.

Whether our time together was a decade or a year or a moment, thank you all.

About the Author

LINA RATHER is a speculative fiction author from Michigan living in Washington, D.C. Her short fiction has appeared in venues including *Lightspeed*, *Fireside*, and *Shimmer*. Her books include *Sisters of the Vast Black,* winner of the Golden Crown Literary Society (Goldie Award) and short-listed for the Theodore Sturgeon Memorial Award, and *Sisters of the Forsaken Stars*. When Lina isn't writing, she likes to cook overly elaborate recipes, read history, and collect cool rocks. Find out more at linarather.com or on Twitter @LinaRather.

TOR·COM

Science fiction. Fantasy. The universe.

And related subjects.

*

More than just a publisher's website, *Tor.com* is a venue for **original fiction, comics,** and **discussion** of the entire field of SF and fantasy, in all media and from all sources. Visit our site today—and join the conversation yourself.

How To
Be
Yourself

Rita
Sherman

HarperSanFrancisco
A Division of HarperCollins Publishers

FIRST EDITION.

LIBRARY OF CONGRESS
CATALOGING·IN·PUBLICATION DATA

Sherman, Rita
  How to be yourself/Rita Sherman
    p. cm
  ISBN 0·06·250772·9
  1. Self· actualization (Psychology) —
Quotations, maxims, etc. 2. Conduct of
life — Quotations, maxims, etc. 3. Aphorisms
and apothegms. I. Title.

BF637.S4552 1992   91·58144
158'.1 — dc20   CIP

  93 94 95 96 HCP·HK 10 9 8 7 6 5 4

This edition is printed on acid·free paper
that meets the American National Standards
Institute Z39.48 Standard. .

To the
memory of
Ronald E. James,
whose dying
changed my living;

and to Chester.

Consider following, rather than leading.

Find your imperatives within.

Always
go to
the heart
of the
matter.

Never wear any-thing tight.

Ask yourself what you would and would not do if you were to learn today you have only six months to live.

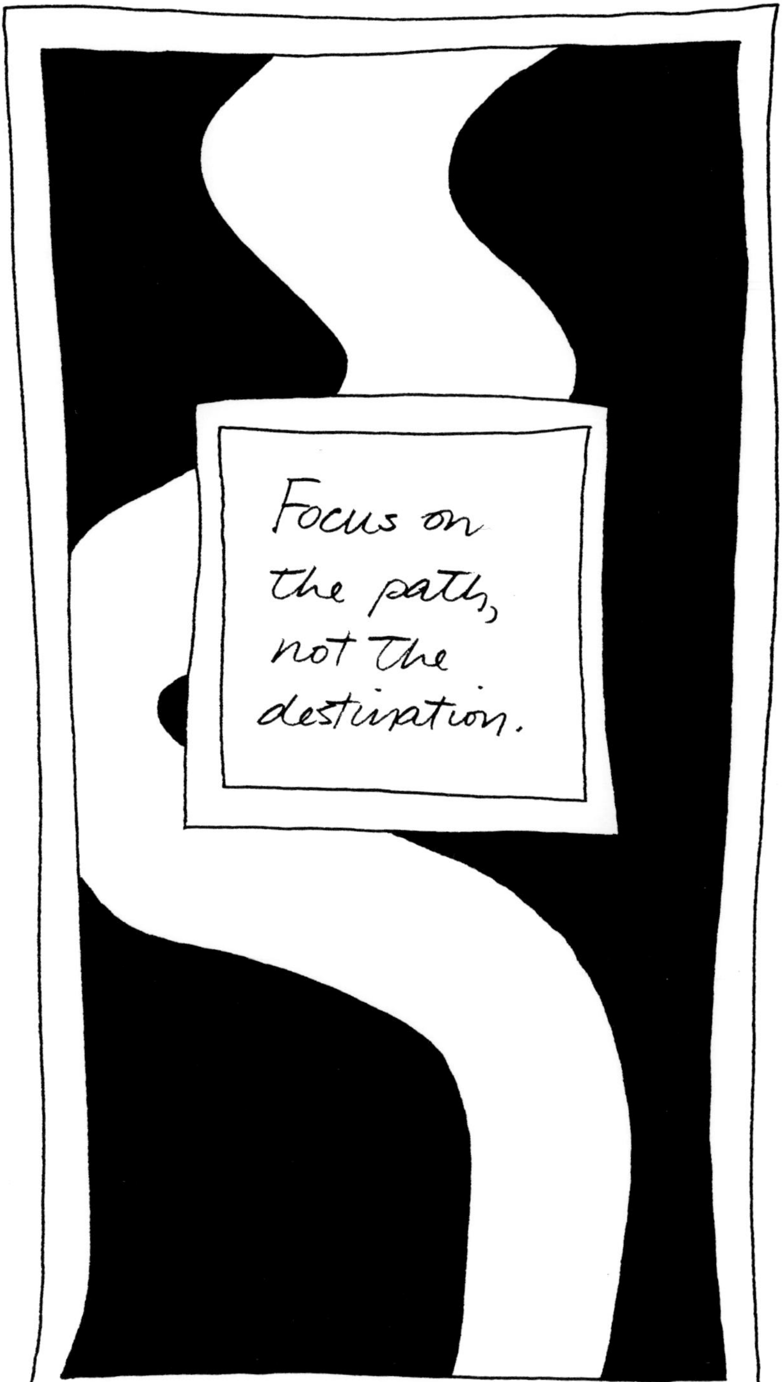
Focus on
the path,
not the
destination.

Understand
that you
do not
understand,
that you
will not
understand,
that you
cannot
understand.

Get enough sleep.

When a little voice inside says "no," don't bully it.

Ask
for
less.

Work
from
the
depths
of
your
being.

Try on careers as you would clothing, until you find one that fits just right.

Never attend an event simply because you've been invited.

Don't
wait
to be
sick
to
take
to
your
bed.

Work
on
emptying,
not
filling.

Take
your
time.

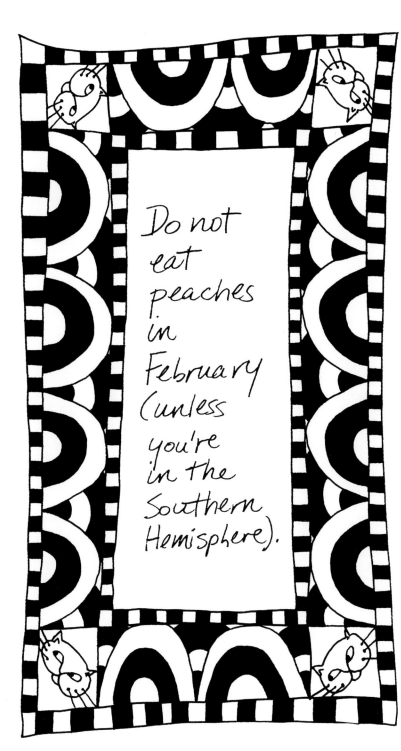

Do not
eat
peaches
in
February
(unless
you're
in the
Southern
Hemisphere).

Pay
attention
to what's
around
you.

Do not
waste.

Don't expect miracles, but be open to them.

Trust your experience.

When you feel unloved, be more loving.

Accept
illness
as
another
gift.

Have faith.

Keep making mistakes.

Never do something today for fear of regretting not having done it tomorrow.

Remember that nobody is a nobody.

Let
your
shame
be
your
teacher.

Appreciate that you need not be guarded to be safe.

Delight
in your
body;
it is
perfect.

When you can't go on any longer, don't.

Give
up
what
you've
never
had.

Do not smile more than is necessary.

Embrace all your feelings, including those you'd rather not have.

Realize that others may be telling you about themselves when they give you advice.

Pursue activities that lead you to forget to eat.

Never enter a contest unless you are prepared to win.

Respect your fallow periods.

Leave room for the un-expected.

Never under—estimate the power of a good joke.

Make the
most
out
of
disaster.

Understand
pain as
your body's
and your
soul's way
of telling
you to
change.

Don't bother trying to be like everyone else; you're not.

(Neither are they.)

Be aware that when you dismiss another person, it is you who is diminished.

false witness against your neighbor. You shall not covet your neighbor's house; you shall not covet your

God blessed the sabbath day and made it holy, ... not do any work—you, your children

God will not clear one who swears ... by His name. Remember the sabbath day and keep it

of the ancestors upon the children ... upon the third and upon the fourth generation? If those who

the heavens above, or on the earth below, or in the waters under the earth. You shall

out of the land of Egypt,

the house of bondage: You shall have no other god besi-

Obey the Ten Command-ments.

God spoke all

do no. ... You shall not make

love, I the ... Love. He ... keep His command-

... Six days shall you labor ...

... your God ... shall not swear falsely by the name of your God; for

... a sculptured image, or any likeness of what is in

these words, saying: I am your God who brought you

Think less about what you do, and more about what you are doing.

Drink
plenty
of
water.

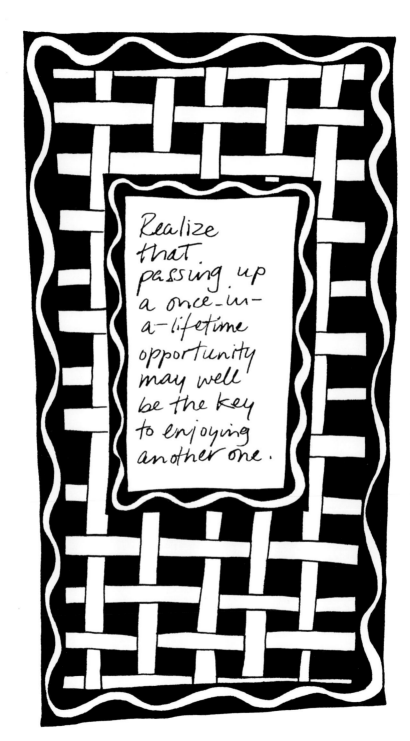

Realize
that
passing up
a once-in-
a-lifetime
opportunity
may well
be the key
to enjoying
another one.

Spend as much time as possible with old people and with children.

When the world seems to be closing in on you take a walk.

Understand that a rejection sometimes spares you something worse later on.

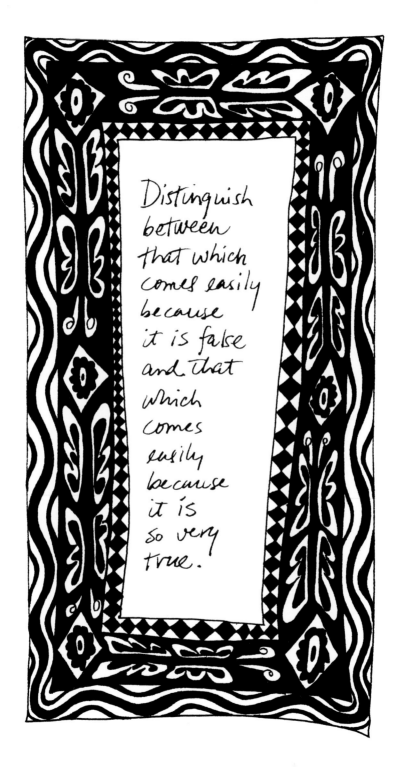

Distinguish between that which comes easily because it is false and that which comes easily because it is so very true.

Never eat a tomato before it's time.

Know that it is what goes on underneath that makes the rest possible.

If good things come before you're ready, imagine what will come when you are.

When
nothing
helps,
do
nothing.

Before you eat, ask yourself what it is you hunger for.

Be careful crossing time zones.

In the
depths
of
winter,
picture
one
perfect
rose.

When
things
look
bad,
read
a good
cookbook.

Before
you
pluck
a flower,
think
about
it.

Practice devotion.

Don't worry about what you are; you are not a what.

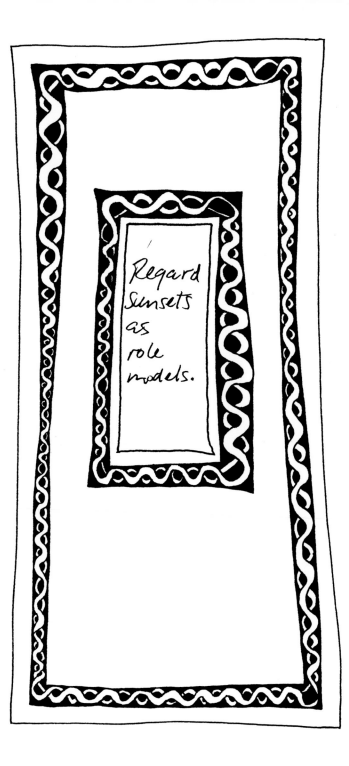

Regard
sunsets
as
role
models.

Appreciate that if you'd done everything "right" in the past, you might not know some of the joys you do today.

Avoid all substances that fool you into thinking you feel better than you do.